So Long at the Park

Dorothy Bodoin

A Wings ePress, Inc.
Mystery Novel

Wings ePress, Inc.

Edited by: Jeanne Smith
Copy Edited by: Christie Kraemer
Executive Editor: Jeanne Smith
Cover Artist: Trisha FitzGerald-Jung

All rights reserved

Names, characters and incidents depicted in this book are products of the author's imagination or are used fictitiously. Any resemblance to actual events, locales, organizations, or persons, living or dead, is entirely coincidental and beyond the intent of the author or the publisher.

No part of this book may be reproduced or transmitted in any form or by any means, electronic or mechanical, including photocopying, recording, or by any information storage and retrieval system, without permission in writing from the publisher.

Wings ePress Books
www.wingsepress.com

Copyright © 2021 by: Dorothy Bodoin
ISBN-13: 978-1-61309-521-8
ISBN-10: 1-61309-521-x

Published In the United States Of America

Wings ePress Inc.
3000 N. Rock Road
Newton, KS 67114

Dedication

To Haywood Clark, my friend and excellent writer's assistant.

* * *

One

An errant breeze stole out of the woods and slipped through the curtain of heat suspended over Woodsboro Park. A refreshing moment in a sweltering spring afternoon, I grabbed it and held on tightly as I sipped my lemonade.

Misty, my white collie, licked her chops. The dogs had their own bottled water, but they knew whatever I was drinking was better. Naturally. Halley and Misty, panting in the meager shade of the lawn chairs, glanced from the cooler to me and back to the cooler.

Sue Appleton, president of the Lakeville Collie League, had unwittingly chosen the hottest day of the year for the first Collie Walkabout in Woodsboro Park. Poor timing, but who could predict the vagaries of a Michigan spring? Still, a little hot spell couldn't keep proud owners from showing off their dogs and exchanging breed, show, and pet talk with like-minded people.

I had enjoyed the camaraderie and happy carnival atmosphere, but after tramping the length of the park twice, I was ready to go home to my green Victorian farmhouse on Jonquil Lane and the air-conditioning.

On the other hand, my friends and I had come to the park as a group, caravanning thirty miles north from Foxglove Corners. Among the party were Annica, a part-time waitress and college student who served as my sometime partner-in-detection, and Brent Fowler, illustrious entrepreneur, fox hunter, and renowned bachelor.

Tagalongs were Molly and Jennifer, teenagers from Sagramore Lake Road, who were helping me with my four collies. Finally, Sue Appleton had brought two young rescues she hoped to place in forever homes.

As I drained my glass of lemonade, Molly and Jennifer emerged from a nearby stand of pine trees. Like most of the young people in the park, they wore short jeans and low-cut tops. Even with their long hair in ponytails, they looked as if they were melting.

"Yikes! It's hot!" Molly turned Velvet's and Gemmy's leashes over to me while Jennifer, holding onto the girls' collie, Ginger, pushed the water bowl closer to Misty's nose.

"I'm glad I'm not wearing a fur coat like you young ladies," she said.

Misty lapped water obligingly, and Halley wagged her tail. Gemmy and Velvet lost no time in stretching out in the shade.

"We just saw the most gorgeous tricolor," Molly announced. "She's *so* beautiful. Her name is Black Rainbow."

"All collies are beautiful." I reached down to give Halley and Velvet a few pats on their heads. They both had gleaming sleek black coats with tan and white markings. Although I had a sable, a blue merle, and a rare bi-black, I had a fondness for the tricolor.

The first collie I remembered seeing as a child was a tri.

"You have to meet this one, Jennet," Jennifer said. "You'll fall in love with her."

"Okay," I said. "Where is she?"

"With her human, Ms. Zoller, by the hot dog stand. Oh, forgive me, pooches. I meant to say by the franks."

I smiled. "They each had a hot dog. We didn't call it by its name."

Molly said, "If you don't catch up to Rainbow, we took her picture."

"We're trying to take pictures of everyone's dog for Sue's album," Jennifer added, "but it's hard. People keep moving around."

I should move, too, before the heat dulled my senses. Eventually, Annica would find me, or Brent, or Sue would. In the meantime, I'd have another glass of lemonade and watch the passing parade.

~ * ~

The feeling stole over me like the breeze from the woods, unbidden and far from welcoming or refreshing. Since moving to Foxglove Corners, I had learned to respect feelings, or forebodings, as I referred to them.

The woods are silent, dark, and deep.

Half of Woodsboro Park, known as the 'old section,' had been in existence for decades with its original slides and swings. The other half consisted of recently donated acreage which included a small lake and a hiking trail through the woods.

It was from the woods behind me that this premonition had drifted.

Something is going to happen soon. Something bad.

What utter nonsense! It didn't take much for me to slide into Melodrama Territory. Sometimes, merely a shift in the collies and people who strolled back and forth in my view. Or a sliver of silence. Or a fleeting impression of a shadow where no shadow should be.

I ignored it.

"Hey, Jennet. Why so serious? This is the most fun I've had in ages."

Annica sank into the spare lawn chair, and her collie, Angel, sat at her feet.

"It's just the heat," I said, admiring the way Annica could wear a white dress and not acquire a single wrinkle or smudge or probably even a dog hair in the course of the day. Her red-gold hair shimmered in the sunlight, and her earrings were tiny ceramic collies with Angel's caramel and white colors.

She poured bottled water into a collapsible bowl for Angel.

"Have you seen Brent?" she asked.

"Not for a while."

"I lost track of him."

That would never do. Annica and Brent had recently reached an understanding of sorts. Any day, I expected to see a diamond engagement ring on her finger.

"He's around somewhere," I said.

Annica settled back in the lawn chair and poured lemonade into a plastic tumbler. "This is collie heaven. Who knew we had so many collies in Foxglove Corners?"

"I'm sure most of them are from other towns," I said.

Sue had advertised the walk widely throughout the southeastern part of the state, hoping to make it an annual event. From what I'd seen so far, it had been a success.

"I wish you could have brought all of your dogs," Annica said.

"So do I. If Crane had been able to come, we would have, but he's on duty."

Which was usually the case. As a deputy sheriff in Foxglove Corners, my husband was more often patrolling the roads and by-roads than at my side for an event or a holiday.

"How did you decide which dogs to bring?" she asked.

"Sky would be miserable in a crowd. Raven never really recovered her stamina after her accident, and Star is elderly. As for Candy, only Crane can control her if she takes it in her head to bolt."

Although they were better off in a cool house, I wished they could all have joined us at the park.

"It's so peaceful here," Annica said. "No customers clamoring for attention, no long reading assignments. Just shade and quiet and collies. Don't you wish you could stay here forever?"

"Good heavens, no!"

I wanted my own home and my collies all together, Crane grilling chicken for dinner, and visits from my neighbor and aunt by marriage, Camille, who considered herself too old for outdoor activities. I imagined her crossing the lane with a fresh baked peach pie, which I'd serve with vanilla ice cream.

"But it's nice for an afternoon," I added. "And I'd come just to see the collies."

Misty tilted her head, then gave a sharp yelp moments before a voice broke the silence with a panicked shout. "Help! Somebody! Help me!"

"Uh-oh. Trouble in paradise. I wonder if someone's dog got loose?"

"It came from over there." I pointed to the woods and rose. "I'll go see, if you'll watch the dogs."

"Go. I'll hold down the fort."

Automatically, I reached for Misty's leash. As Annica was my partner-in-detection, the pretty tri-headed white collie was my canine sidekick. Based on past experiences, I believed she had a subtle psychic streak.

Not that anything out of the ordinary was going on. Someone's dog had slipped out of his leash and was running free in the park. It happened.

Still, there was that warning carried on the breeze.

I led Misty into the group that had quickly formed to answer the cry for help.

"What's up, Jennet?"

Brent Fowler stepped out of the rushing crowd. Hearing a well-loved voice, Misty circled around his feet, almost entangling him in her leash. Picturing him sprawled on the ground, an accidental victim of the Collie Walkabout, I held out a hand to steady him.

"Thanks," he said. "What do you think happened?"

"Nothing good."

Most of the activity in the park centered around the cleared space at the entrance, currently crowded with crates, lawn chairs, tents, and temporary stands. Alongside a pen stood a young woman with long auburn hair and a tricolor collie. Not an unusual sight at the Collie Walkabout, but she looked as though she were on the verge of hysterics.

I'd seen her somewhere, but she'd looked different. Then I remembered a serene young lady in a short, beaded dress with a flapper's saucy bob. She worked at the Green House of Antiques. I couldn't remember her name.

"Rainbow!" she wailed. "Where are you?"

The collie dog sat at her side, ears flattened against her head, a study in dejection. She looked more upset than her owner.

Always ready to help a damsel in distress, Brent went up to her. "What's the matter, miss? Can we help?"

"Someone stole my dog," she cried.

Two

I moved closer to Brent and the distraught young woman. The collie's ears seemed to vanish in sleek black fur. I held my hand under her nose and, when she trained her dark soulful eyes on me, stroked her head. I couldn't remember when I'd seen such a display of canine misery.

"I don't understand," I said. "You're saying this isn't your dog?"

She let the leash fall to the ground. "I never saw this animal before, but it's wearing Rainbow's collar and tags. It was in Rainbow's crate."

It? The tri was a female, on the small side, pretty, and obviously traumatized.

"I was just talking to my friends," the woman said. "Just for a minute. I wasn't watching Rainbow. I thought it was safe. It *should* have been safe."

The situation she described was difficult to comprehend. How could one dog be substituted for another with hundreds of people milling around to bear witness to any nefarious doings? It didn't make sense.

The door to the crate was open. A large green ball had rolled to a stop in a corner, waiting for its owner. Beside it, a stainless steel water bowl was almost empty. The sight tugged at my heart.

I surveyed the crowd, intending to ask if anyone had been seen lurking around Rainbow's pen, but most of the onlookers had melted into the background. Sobered by the mystifying apparent dognapping, all were keeping eagles' eyes on their own collies and strong hands on their leashes. I imagined their thoughts were similar: *I'm glad it didn't happen to me.*

One who remained, a chunky woman whose green polka dot sundress struggled to cover her body, pushed her sunglasses high into her upswept blonde hair.

"You'd better call the cops," she said. "That's what I'd be doing if my dog went missing."

"The police, yes, I will." Rainbow's owner pulled her phone out of her purse, but instead frowned at me. "Don't I know you?"

"From the Green House of Antiques," I said. "I'm one of your best customers."

"Now I remember. You're always looking for those old mystery books. I'm Ellalyn Zoller."

She stooped to retrieve the leash of the collie who had remained steadfastly by her side. "Now what am I going to do with this one?"

The dog who wasn't Rainbow.

"Put her in the crate for now," I suggested. Noticing a six pack of bottled water on top of the pen, I added, "And get her a fresh drink. She's panting."

"Hold off on calling the police," Brent said. "Maybe we can find your dog. I see a couple of black collies over there."

"So do I, but they're not mine."

"Would Rainbow have gone with a stranger?" I asked, thinking of my own collies. Candy, for one, would never let herself be taken away from me.

"She might have," Ellalyn said. "She loves people."

Leading a pair of bouncy young sables, Sue Appleton broke through what remained of the crowd that had gathered around Ellalyn. "What happened? Jennet?"

"Someone snatched my collie," Ellalyn said. "She was resting in her crate. I looked away just for a minute."

She added details, mostly variations on the theme. In the retelling, the story sounded like a grim fairy tale enacted in a twenty-first century park. A malevolent fairy steals a collie and leaves a changeling in her place.

But we were dealing with real life, with an invisible thief who was somehow able to carry out his bold plan in a densely populated park without being observed.

How much time would it have taken him to remove Rainbow's collar, put it on the other dog, and get away? And did the thief think Rainbow's owner wouldn't notice?

The scenario seemed impossible, but I resisted going back to the fairy theory.

Not yet ready to accept what had happened on her watch, Sue said, "Your dog may not be gone, Ms. Zoller, only misplaced."

Sue glanced at me for help. I shrugged.

"This could be someone's idea of a sick joke," she said. "Do you have any enemies?"

She hesitated. "I don't think so. No. Of course not."

Sue said, "I'll post a guard on the parking lot. No one will leave unless they can prove they're taking their own dog. I know many of the people here. Meanwhile, we'll get a search party together."

Brent took my arm. "Jennet and I will follow the hiking trail to the lake."

Out of the heat, cooled by a thick canopy of leaves over our heads, a shadowy, secretive route. Misty insisted on investigating every new enticing scent that came her way. I let her stop but kept a tight hold on her lead.

As soon as we were out of earshot, Brent said, "It doesn't look good."

"No, it doesn't."

"Dogs don't vanish from closed crates."

"Not unless they have help."

But this was a mere thirty miles from Foxglove Corners, Home of the Strange and the Vanished.

As we hurried down the trail, I glanced on either side. No one had cleared the donated property. Possibly they'd leave it in its current wild state and perhaps widen the path.

The woods were silent, dark, and deep. They would make a good hiding place. Was Rainbow there hiding with her abductor in the dark beneath the trees?

"I don't see how that could have happened," Brent said. "I wonder if the Zoller girl is making it up."

"I don't think so. She seemed genuinely distressed and baffled. Besides, what would be the point?"

By now, of course, I had dismissed the idea of rapacious fairy folk and a changeling. Well, maybe not the changeling. This was the work of a person who knew exactly how to strike at the heart of their victim.

Through her dog.

And what of the collie who had taken Rainbow's place? Where was her owner? Where was her home?

What if somebody had taken one of my precious collies?

I became conscious of an overwhelming desire to walk in the sun.

"I am half sick of shadows," I said.

~ * ~

"Hey, guys. Wait up."

Molly and Jennifer had followed us, ever eager to be part of an adventure, even one with tragic undertones. They looked as fresh and energetic as if they'd just entered the park.

Ah, to be young again!

"Where's Ginger?" I asked.

"Annica's watching everyone," Jennifer said. "We want to help find Rainbow for Ms. Zoller."

"Jennifer and I can search the woods," Molly added.

"That's a bad idea. We don't want to start looking for two lost girls."

"Really, Jennet," Jennifer said. "We can take care of ourselves, and Rainbow knows us."

But they agreed to stay with us on the hiking trail.

It ended in a stretch of beach and a sky-blue lake awash in light. Because of the heat, I expected to find the area crowded, but only a single man walked his collie on the sand. It was a mahogany sable whose coat had an ethereal shine in the sunlight. Jennifer ran ahead to ask him if he'd seen a black collie. I could tell by their body language that he hadn't.

"What now?" she asked.

"We'd better head back," Brent said. "Maybe Rainbow came home."

"She didn't let herself out of her crate," I pointed out.

"Then maybe someone brought her back."

At the park entrance, Lieutenant Mac Dalby of the Foxglove Corners Police Department had taken charge. He was a tall, handsome officer with cornflower blue eyes and a condescending streak that often targeted me for some imaginary infraction.

Not today, though. I recalled that Mac loved dogs. As a boy, he'd had a collie.

"I have two men scouring the woods," he announced, "but it looks like whoever took the dog made a clean getaway."

"Don't say that," Ellalyn said.

She hadn't held up well. Her eye makeup was smudged, and her hair tangled. She fussed with it constantly, pushing wayward strands back from her face and twisting them around her fingers.

"I came here with my dog, and I'm not leaving without her," she said, as if that bold statement could negate reality.

"You can't stay in the park," Sue said. "It won't be safe when everybody leaves."

"How safe was it with everybody here?" she countered.

No one had an answer for her.

We would all have to go home soon. We still had plenty of light left in the day, but some people had driven long distances to attend the collie event. Sensing that the drama had wound down to an unresolved end, many had already drifted away.

"I want my dog," Ellalyn said.

"I know." Again Sue looked at me.

I had to say something encouraging. "We haven't found her yet, but..."

"But we will," Brent insisted. "Jennet's an ace at solving mysteries. She's a top-notch girl detective."

I glared at him.

Ellalyn attempted a smile, a weak effort indeed. It didn't match the deepening despair in her eyes.

"I should have known that from all those mystery books you buy," she said.

Three

One matter remained unresolved. The tricolor collie who wasn't Rainbow. The changeling; the unwanted one. She lay in her crate, her head resting on her paws, her plight reaching out for my heart.

No one had come forward to claim her, which presented us with a problem. Yes, us. I couldn't walk away from Ellalyn like the others, whose attention had waned when it appeared that nothing else of note was going to happen.

Neither could Brent nor Sue who was, after all, the president of the Collie Rescue League.

Ellalyn was getting ready to leave. She emptied the water bowl on the ground. "I'll come back tomorrow," she said. "I want to be here if they bring Rainbow back."

They? Surely the theft was the work of one person, and I doubted that whoever had stolen Rainbow would return her.

"Will you take this other dog with you?" Sue asked.

Ellalyn was quick with her answer. "Why would I do that? She doesn't belong to me."

"That's true, but..." Usually Sue radiated confidence, but the day's bizarre happening had left her floundering. "Her owner doesn't seem to be here. We can't just leave her on her own in the park."

Ellalyn opened the crate door and said, "Come out now, black dog." She reached inside for Rainbow's ball. The collie didn't stir.

A little bit of the sympathy I'd felt for Ellalyn slipped away. The collie's origin might be a mystery, but she was a sentient being, a sweet, frightened changeling. A dog in the wrong place at the wrong time through no fault of her own.

"I'm with collie rescue," Sue said as if to remind herself of her responsibility. "I'll take her home with me."

"She'll need a name," Brent pointed out. "Anyone, any ideas?"

"Pepper?" I said.

He frowned. "That's too common for a tri. How about Piper? Or Pippa?"

"Pepper," I repeated. "It's only temporary. Her owner may turn up."

So I said, but I thought it unlikely. The little tri had been a pawn in a cruel game. But with Sue she was in good hands. If by chance her owner never turned up, Sue would place her in a home where she would be wanted. Who wouldn't love such a winsome little creature?

A pall seemed to settle over the park as the crowd dwindled down to small clusters of collie owners dismantling tents and pens and makeshift refreshment stands. A smell of popcorn lingered in the air, reminding me that I was hungry. A blue balloon sailed by, its long string trailing behind.

Somewhere two dogs were barking, but mostly the park had fallen silent. So silent it might be in the grip of a spell. I shivered as I recalled my premonition. The image of a prowling fairy searching for a collie to steal insinuated itself in my mind.

But I wasn't going to indulge in flights of fancy.

Ellalyn and I exchanged addresses and phone numbers, and I assured her that we weren't deserting her, that we would try to find out what had happened to Rainbow. Then slowly, Brent, Annica, Sue, and I gathered our collies and walked to the parking lot together. Jennifer and Molly had already left with Molly's dad.

"Until this happened, everything was going so well," Sue said. "Now all people will remember about this event is that a dog disappeared under mysterious circumstances."

I wished I could think of something to say that would make her feel better, but nothing came to mind.

After all, she was right. It takes a long time, maybe forever, for an unfortunate occurrence to disassociate itself from the place where it happened.

"Tomorrow's Sunday," Brent said. "Let's meet for breakfast around ten, whoever can, and make a plan."

"At Clovers," Annica added. "I don't have to work. It'll be fun letting someone else wait on me."

I helped Halley into the back seat of our new SUV and once again, counted my dogs. I'd brought four collies to the Walkabout; I was taking four home. One couldn't be too careful or complacent.

"Clovers it is," I said. "Till tomorrow morning then."

~ * ~

Home was a green Victorian farmhouse on Jonquil Lane with a stained glass window between graceful double gables, and four barking dogs vying for space in the front window. Home was a pizza on the kitchen counter, and a tall deputy sheriff with frosty gray eyes and silver streaks in his blond hair waiting for me. Home was here.

"Did you all have fun at the collie walk, honey?" Crane asked.

"We did until something weird happened. I'll fill you in later."

The four travelling canines pounced on their water bowl and promptly found their favorite places to rest. Candy stationed herself as close to the pizza as she could possibly get, while I went upstairs for a quick shower.

I came back down wearing a fresh white dress and began to toss a salad while Crane set the table and fed the dogs.

I told him about Rainbow vanishing from her crate and our unsuccessful search of the park.

How unlikely the story sounded! Before I could stop myself, I added my first thought about thieving fairies and changelings.

Crane said, "The dog's owner claimed she was just distracted for a few minutes?"

"So she said."

"I wonder. It could have been longer. She either didn't realize how much time was passing, or she's trying to unload some of her guilt."

"It does seem like a lot to happen in a few minutes," I said. "Apparently, nobody saw anything out of the ordinary. Or they may have thought someone was giving one of their dogs a rest and taking the other out for exercise."

"It was obviously planned," he added.

I nodded. "To the last detail, which was to leave Pepper in Rainbow's place."

"I assume you volunteered to help Rainbow's owner find her," Crane said.

He knew me well. "I love really impossible mysteries. They're so much more challenging than the ones where you have to try to figure out who done it with a handful of motivated suspects."

"Ones from the Twilight Zone?"

"Exactly."

Candy crept closer to the pizza and gave me a 'hurry up' woof. I lit the tapers in our treasured antique candlesticks that had belonged to Crane's Civil War-era ancestress, Rebecca Ferguson, and checked to see that the tumblers and pitcher of iced tea were in place.

"My mysteries are almost always dog-centered," I said. "We're all going to help find Rainbow. Brent, Annica, Sue, of course, and Molly and Jennifer."

"With a team like that, you can't lose."

Crane was, without a doubt, my greatest fan.

I gave the salad a final stir, and we sat at the table while Candy and Velvet settled themselves in the doorway to wait for the best part of the meal.

Leftover crust.

Four

The painted clover chain that bordered the little restaurant on Crispian Road had a mesmerizing green shimmer in the light. It was one of those lazy, delicious mornings that you wish would last forever. Even the clover chimes on the door sang a happier song.

Seeing I was the last to arrive, I bypassed the dessert carousel with only a cursory glance and slipped into a seat beside Annica.

I had cooked a hearty breakfast for Crane but had only a piece of toast with a cup of tea myself. I wanted to be hungry for a stack of pancakes drenched in maple syrup. Or maybe French toast.

Brent said, "I can't get Rainbow out of my mind. How in the hell could anyone take her out of that crate without being seen?"

"And out of the park," Annica added. "Don't forget that."

Sue said, "It was crowded, but people were busy with their own dogs and conversations, and she was close to the entrance."

"Since we don't know how this happened, I suggest we concentrate on who did it," I said. "I suspect it was a personal strike against Ellalyn Zoller."

Annica leaned forward, her coffee momentarily forgotten. "It'll be fun. Let's see who can find Rainbow first. We'll make a game out of it."

"Don't forget, this is Ellalyn's life," I said. "Her sorrow."

"So, what do we do?"

"Start with Ellalyn. We need to know all about her. She said she doesn't have enemies, but she must have."

We all did. Even I had given a few villains good reason to seek revenge.

"Could it be that somebody wanted Rainbow for some reason?" Sue asked. "We need to know her history. Maybe she's a valuable show prospect."

Remembering her coffee, Annica took a long sip and dabbed at her lips. "How can you show a dog you don't own?"

"With subterfuge," I said. "Forged papers?"

If that were the thief's motivation. For some reason, I doubted it.

Had that ever happened? Was Rainbow microchipped? I drew my mystery notebook out of my purse, and jotted down a few notes and questions to myself. At this point, I welcomed any scrap of information, no matter how outrageous it seemed at first glance.

"I really need to talk to Ellalyn," I said. "She may have answers she's unaware of."

"What can I do to help?" Annica asked.

"The usual," I said. "Call shelters. Put up flyers. The girls took Rainbow's picture just before she vanished. That'll help."

Sue said, "I'll post a 'lost dog' notice on my Facebook collie pages."

"And I'll ask Ellalyn if Rainbow has any distinctive markings." That reminded me of our little changeling, a tricolor with a full white ruff. "By the way, how is Pepper doing?"

"Well enough. She doesn't seem to be happy, though. Bluebell tries to play with her, but she'd rather be alone. I don't think Pepper likes me," she added.

"You're imagining it," Brent said. "Everybody likes you. Especially the dogs."

I pictured a dog taken from her home, if that was how the thief had acquired her.

"Pepper may be mourning for the life she was used to. Where did she live before she turned up in Rainbow's pen wearing her collar?"

That, of course, was part of the mystery. Did she belong to the person who had spirited Rainbow out of the park? One incident and dozens of unknowns.

"I can't wait to get started," Annica announced.

As if on cue, Marcy appeared, order pad in hand.

I was willing to wait. A good breakfast would fortify me for what came next.

~ * ~

And school came second, although it was an entire day away.

The rest of Sunday flew by as if it had wings. I called Ellalyn, hoping to arrange a meeting with her but had to leave a message on her voice mail.

While dinner was in the oven, I glanced at the *Banner,* surprised to find that Jill Lodge, cousin of the paper's owner, Cameron, had written a brief article about Rainbow's disappearance during the collie event. The only new information was the mention of a twelve-hundred dollar reward for Rainbow's safe return.

That generous amount might entice a person with knowledge of the crime to contact the police. The dognapper himself might be tempted to return Rainbow, claiming to have found her.

After dinner, I stacked my schoolwork on the kitchen counter so it would be ready to grab in the morning on my way out to the car. The last days of school before summer vacation were always chaotic. I intended to be ready for them.

~ * ~

I didn't expect the confetti mess in the halls, though. Surely it was too early to be tearing notepaper into tiny pieces and discarding workbooks. Most classes were still reviewing for final exams. I felt as if we were walking into a carnival without the music.

Wait! Here came the blare of a popular tune from a boom box.

Leonora skidded on a patch of shredded maps and grabbed my arm.

"It's going to be a wild day," she said.

Sweltering summertime weather worked against us, an early heat wave bringing visions of sun and water that were more powerful than anything the school could offer. In fact, many students were dressed as if they were bound for the beach rather than a classroom.

Principal Grimsley had instructed us to send students to the office if they disregarded Marston's approved dress code, but if we did that, the office would be overrun, and the classrooms all but empty. Besides, being dismissed from class might well be a student's goal.

Stroll past the office, breathe the enticing summery air. Walk the freedom trail.

"I expect you teachers to set a good example," he had said at our last staff meeting while fingering his red, white, and blue tie as if were choking him.

I felt my sleeveless navy polka dot dress did that admirably. Furthermore, the material was cool and floaty.

Unless someone came to class attired in a swimsuit, I planned to ignore shorts and tank tops.

With that in mind, I concentrated on reviewing a semester's worth of material in all classes, confiscated two forbidden water pistols, and wished I had a soft drink. Tea, lemonade, Vernor's ginger ale—anything with chunks of ice floating in it. My students were wilting, too listless to do anything of significance.

The day progressed without incident until the last class of the day arrived. I was taking attendance. A young man with a vaguely familiar face occupied the last desk in the sixth row, one that was usually empty. It had been assigned to Russell (Rusty) Delmar, a boy who had been absent for so many weeks I'd assumed he'd dropped the class and I'd lost the paperwork.

But there he was, elbow leaning on his literature textbook looking quite at home.

"Rusty Delmar? Where did you come from?"

He smirked and looked at his classmates for approval. "Around," he said. "Here and there."

No one reacted.

"Can I have my make-up work?" he asked.

I stared at him. "Your make-up work? You've been gone for weeks."

"Yeah. So, can I have it?"

"You've missed the entire course," I pointed out. "Well, almost."

"Yeah, but I can make it up."

"And you could have attended class every day, too," I said.

"Just write down what I missed," he said. "I'll put it on your desk tomorrow."

"I don't think I can do that."

"You have to," he said. "You're the teacher."

You've heard of a line in the sand. Rusty had just drawn one. It was so clear, I could practically see it, could almost feel its grit on my tongue. More than ever, I longed for that cold drink.

I could, of course, make a list of all the assignments I'd given during the semester, together with the reading material, but to do so would be wrong. What would that say to all the students who had been in class every day, participating in discussion?

Besides, wasn't there a policy about a certain number of unexcused absences resulting in an automatic failure? I thought so but would have to check. My first step would be to have a talk with Rusty's counselor.

Drat. I knew this day was going too well.

"I'll let you know," I said and began handing out review sheets.

Five

The bell rang, and my fifth hour students exited the room with a maximum amount of noise. As sixth period was my conference hour, the school day was as good as over for me. I locked the door and set out to visit Rusty's counselor, Joyce Gillyard.

The halls were empty and eerily silent, and, at present, Joyce was alone in the counselors' office. Her cubicle had a soothing view of the courtyard with its fountain spilling water from the statue's vessel.

Joyce sat in front of a floor fan staring at a stack of forms, doing nothing with them that I could see. She looked fairly cool and definitely unwilted in powder blue with a white bead necklace, her silvery hair held back by a matching cloth band. A can of Coca-Cola sat on her desk, alongside a tall glass of bottled water.

Oh, for the life of a counselor!

"I'd like to talk to you about Russell Delmar." I pulled one of the chairs over to her desk. "He showed up in my American Lit class today. He's been absent for weeks."

"Russell," she said. "He's constantly on the unexcused absence list. I've tried to reach his mother several times."

And given up, I supposed. I didn't have that luxury.

"He wants me to give him make-up work," I said. "Weeks and weeks of it."

She nodded. "It must have just dawned on him that he needs to pass your class if he wants to graduate."

That was news, and unwelcome news at that. I had assumed Rusty was a junior. I watched the stakes rise before my eyes. The seniors' last day was a week away.

"He should have realized that back in January," I said.

"I agree."

"Isn't there a policy about a certain number of unexcused absences resulting in an automatic failure?" I asked.

"Depending on circumstances," Joyce said. "A student with a serious illness could have assignments sent home."

"That doesn't apply in Rusty's case."

"Not at all."

"What was he doing when he should have been in class, I wonder."

Joyce shrugged. "Who knows what he was up to? He's repeating the course. The material should have been a snap."

And possibly he found it boring, but no matter.

"Well, he's not going to get credit from me for a class he blew off," I said.

In other words, I wasn't going to give him the make-up work he'd demanded.

"I'll have a talk with Russell," Joyce said. "And I'll try to get in touch with his mother."

She should have discussed his progress or lack thereof long before this, but it wasn't my place to tell her how to do her job.

"Thanks, and stay cool. Let me know what you find out," I added.

I wasn't naive enough to think Joyce could make the matter go away. It was back in my lap; it had never left.

In my room, I tidied my desk, separating material I wanted to take home from the general clutter. This activity usually had the effect of energizing me, but today it didn't. With the semester almost over, I didn't need a thorny problem to solve, but it appeared I didn't have a choice.

I sighed, my thoughts returning to my other life, the one away from Marston High School. Finding a stolen collie would be a breeze compared to dealing with an entitled brat who expected something for nothing. When he graduated, if he did, he would have a shattering wake up call.

I knew what I was going to do, knew what was right. Still, I suspected I could benefit from allies. Did Grimsley know about Rusty's dilemma? And would he side with me? Or (horrors) with him?

Don't make a serious problem worse, I told myself.

~ * ~

Although long, our commute was pleasant and even relaxing once we exited the freeway. It was mostly woods with green leaves that hadn't yet been burned by a summer sun or nibbled by the inevitable insects, and a profusion of wildflowers added vibrant color to the landscape. Admittedly, the scene was even more enjoyable when viewed from inside an air-cooled vehicle.

"It's too hot to cook tonight," Leonora said. "Let's stop at Clovers for take-out."

"Great idea. I hope they have some good desserts left. I'd like a strawberry pie."

Leonora had changed dramatically from the new bride who would happily prepare a home-cooked meal from scratch for her husband, Jake, even in a heat wave. I took credit for pointing out the advantages of relying on Mary Jeanne, Clover's owner and cook, in an emergency.

Neither Crane nor Jake, to my knowledge, had ever complained about being served restaurant food. But then, Clovers was no ordinary restaurant.

"Annica should be working this afternoon," I said. "She's only taking one course this spring."

Sometimes I dreamed about being a college student again, young and idealistic, attending lectures, taking notes, and discovering literature that transported me to new realms. No discipline problems, no untoward noise and chaos, no difficult decisions to make. It had been heaven.

But it was a passing fantasy, nothing more. I didn't have a time machine, and besides, I liked my career. Most of the time, especially at this time of the year with long weeks of vacation spread out before us. Infinite possibilities and a chance to start anew in the fall.

And a new mystery to solve.

~ * ~

Was it my imagination or were the painted clovers that bordered the little restaurant wilting?

A touch of the light, I decided as we plowed through a wall of stagnant heat. A few minutes, a few steps, and we were inside being revived by artificial air.

"I'd like a cold drink," Leonora said. "A tall glass of ice tea or..."

"A lime cooler." That drink was a summertime special invented by Annica, who closely guarded her recipe.

All in sunny yellow and crisp white, she emerged from the kitchen carrying a tray of lemon tarts and chocolate iced brownies. We stopped by the dessert carousel as she placed the confections in the empty spaces.

"Hi, girls. You just missed Ellalyn Zoller," she said. "She left about five minutes ago."

"Is there any news about Rainbow?" I asked.

"She's still missing, and Ellalyn looks like she's coming apart at the seams."

"Poor girl," Leonora murmured. "Poor Rainbow."

"She tells me that ever since Rainbow vanished, she's been driving around Foxglove Corners looking for her. She went back to Woodsboro Park several times."

"That was three days ago," I pointed out.

"She left a flyer for us to put up. I'll have to ask Mary Jeanne, but I'm sure she'll be okay with it. She likes dogs."

Her tray empty, Annica led us to my favorite booth with the best view of the Crispian Road woods.

"Just driving around," Leonora said. "That doesn't seem like a productive way to find a lost dog."

"It's better than sitting at home, waiting."

"She had a cup of coffee and a roll," Annica said. "She says she's lost her appetite."

"Understandable."

"But she looked thinner and, well, not healthy. Can you lose weight in three days?"

"I never could. We promised to help her, but she never called me back. I'll call her again tonight."

A grim possibility tugged at me. If Rainbow's abductor had taken her out of the county, all of Ellalyn's wanderings through Foxglove Corners and the wilds of Woodsboro Park were a waste of time.

I had to come up with a better plan. But we'd already done everything I could think of.

Six

The next day, I dropped Leonora off at her house, made a quick stop at home to take care of the dogs, then met Ellalyn Zoller at Clovers. She wore an apricot flapper's dress with a rope of shimmering pearls that dropped down to her waist. Explaining that she'd just finished her shift at the Green House of Antiques, she seemed oblivious of the admiring glances that came her way.

"They like Lola and me to advertise the vintage clothes and tell people where to buy them," she said, as she smoothed her necklace over the beaded bodice. "But I'm not about to trip myself in one of those long skirts, especially on such a hot day. This dress is comfortable."

"It's pretty," I said. And Ellalyn looked lovely in it, not the coming-apart wraith of Annica's description. "I love vintage dresses."

We ordered lime coolers, and I opened my mystery notebook to a new page. "Is there any word about Rainbow?"

"Not a thing. I've been looking for her every chance I have."

"Looking where?" I asked.

"All around Foxglove Corners. Every day I take a new route home, and I've been back to the Woodsboro Park three times."

"Why the park?"

"One night, I dreamed Rainbow was still there. She was crying. Looking for me.

"That's unlikely," I said. "If she were there, somebody would have seen her or heard her. But I know how real dreams can be."

Ellalyn grasped a handful of pearls and held them as if they were a lifeline. "I was hoping the reward would help."

"Jennifer and Molly have flooded the area with flyers," I said. "They illustrated them with a picture of Rainbow taken just before she vanished."

"For all the good it did."

"Don't lose hope. It hasn't been a week yet, and it's been so hot. People may be staying in their homes with the air conditioning. My husband is a deputy sheriff," I added. "He's looking, too. You have a lot of people on your side."

"And I appreciate it. I do. But I want Rainbow back. At least I haven't come across a collie's body. I didn't think I would. Someone took her away."

Marcy set our lime coolers on the table. I swirled the straw through the minty green liquid, dispersing the whipped cream, and took a long, long sip. This was my favorite summer drink, but I'd never been able to replicate it.

Ellalyn said, "I've always been afraid of woods. It goes back to my childhood. Hansel and Gretel, you know. Getting lost. Being shoved into a witch's oven."

That image had also traumatized my five-year-old self.

"Children's stories can be scary," I said.

"So can life."

"If Rainbow were still in the park, don't you think she'd have come when you called her?"

"If she could. I'm thinking she might have been prevented. Whoever stole her would have to keep her quiet."

"On Saturday, maybe, but surely she's been moved by now."

Ellalyn twisted her necklace into a knot. I opened my notebook and looked in my purse for my pen.

"Tell me about Rainbow," I said. "She's young…"

"She'll be eight months old next week. She's just a puppy."

"Where did you acquire her?"

"From Lily Carrey at Springbrook Kennels out of Maple Falls. I wanted a female, a tri, but couldn't find one. Lily was expecting a winter litter. I asked her to put me on her waiting list. I bought Rainbow without even seeing her picture. She was everything I hoped for."

"Does Lily know Rainbow was stolen?" I asked.

"I called her right away. Not that I suspect her, not really, but I think she wanted to keep Rainbow. The other pups were males or blues. I don't know." She paused, took a sip of her drink, gazed out at the woods across the road. "Do you think Lily might be behind this?"

"I doubt it."

I couldn't imagine a breeder stealing back a puppy she'd sold. If anything, she would have retracted her promise to Ellalyn. But I couldn't imagine that happening either, not with an ethical breeder.

Still, I jotted down *Lily Carrey, Springbrook, Maple Falls,* in my notebook. It would be interesting to know who'd bought the rest of Rainbow's littermates. Unfortunately, the kennel was located up north, about a four-hour drive away.

"I don't know Lily well, just from her website, but I'm grasping at straws," Ellalyn said. "All straws."

"The other day at the park you said you didn't have any enemies," I reminded her. "Are you sure about that?"

She looked startled, even offended, but she said, "I get along with people. I lead a quiet life. When I bought Rainbow, I joined a collie club and took a puppy obedience class, but I'm not a joiner. I just wanted my precious collie. Just her and me. Now I'm alone again."

"If you don't mind answering a personal question, is there a man in your life?"

She looked away, contemplating the view from the window. "Not at present. No, there's no one."

I sketched a heart and a question mark in my notebook. It wasn't unheard of for a jealous or disgruntled lover to try to hurt a woman through her dog. But I had to take Ellalyn at her word— until I had reason to doubt her. There was that hesitation.

"There's no one to envy you?" I asked. "No one would want to own Rainbow?"

"That's bizarre," she said. "Just because I couldn't find a tricolor when I wanted one doesn't mean they're not available. Whoever stole Rainbow could buy his own dog from another breeder."

"Don't forget," I said. "This was personal. It was well-planned. The thief watched you and waited for a moment when you were distracted. He had the other tri ready. He removed Rainbow's leash, left Pepper in Rainbow's place, and spirited your dog away."

"It's fiendish," she said.

"But it happened."

"I'll swear I only looked away for maybe five minutes."

"You'd think the switch would have taken longer," I said. "It all went off like clockwork."

Running out of ideas, I tossed out an unlikely question. "How about one of your customers at the Green House?"

She stared at me. "They're just customers, Jennet. I don't know them. None of them knows me or anything about my life. Only you."

Reluctantly, I closed my notebook.

"I want to find Rainbow for you," I said, "but I don't have much to go on."

A cleverly orchestrated theft in a crowded park. A young woman who lived quietly with her dog, who impressed me as being nice and quite ordinary. If I were to believe her, she had no vengeful boyfriend in her past. No enemy...

Enemy?

A thought jolted through my thoughts, and my perception shifted. Could Rainbow be the one with the enemy?

A sweet collie girl—weren't they all sweet?—not even a year old?

Preposterous.

Still...

Leave no stone unturned, I told myself. *Not even the Springbrook connection.*

Or...Was it possible the answer to the mystery could be found in the dark woods of Ellalyn's childhood imagination? A tempting edible cottage containing a blazing oven? In Woodsboro Park?

Double preposterous.

The sun has gotten to you, I told myself, and finished my lime cooler.

Seven

Brent visited us that evening in time for dinner, a pot roast with potatoes and carrots, everybody's favorite, and the one dish I could create that rivaled a Clovers' entree. Over coffee and orange chiffon cake from my own oven, he said, "I asked the girls to change the flyers to reflect the new reward for Rainbow's safe return."

"To how much?" I asked.

"I tacked on an extra thousand."

That would bring the amount to twenty-two hundred dollars, surely enough to tempt the thief or a greedy informant.

"Did you make any headway with Ellalyn Zoller?" he asked.

"Nothing outstanding," I said. "Ellalyn is exactly what she appears to be—a girl who took her collie to the Walkabout."

"There has to be more to it," Crane pointed out.

"Yes, but what?"

"You're the detective," Brent reminded me.

"When school's out, I may drive up to Maple Falls and talk to Rainbow's breeder," I said.

Crane accepted the coffee refill I poured him. "Not alone. It's too dangerous."

"Not dangerous, but a long solitary drive is no fun. I'll ask Annica to go with me and take one of the dogs. Misty, I think."

From her seat on Brent's lap, Misty heard her name. She tilted her head.

Misty, my psychic collie. This mystery could benefit from a little supernatural help.

"Was Rainbow's breeder at the park on Saturday?" Brent asked.

"I don't know. I never met her. Maybe Sue can tell me."

Crane frowned. "As a suspect, she doesn't sound promising, honey. Why would a breeder steal back her own puppy?"

I'd asked myself the same question and couldn't think of a reason. If the breeder didn't want to part with Rainbow, why not simply tell Ellalyn she'd changed her mind and offer her another puppy, perhaps at a discount to compensate for Ellalyn's disappointment?

Disappointment. That was the key word. Ellalyn had fallen in love with Rainbow from her breeder's description. In her view, Rainbow was as good as hers, even before she was ready to go to her new home. A substitute would be unacceptable.

I always wanted a black collie. I waited for years. Finally...

Eight months of happiness with the perfect dog, not even a full year of dreams come true; then she was gone. Like a child snatched from her safe place at a heavily-attended collie event.

"I won't say Ellalyn is deliberately misleading us, but maybe there's something she doesn't consider significant," I said.

"Are you going to see her again?" Brent asked.

"We'll get together on Saturday for lunch, but I thought I'd talk to one of her friends first."

"About her? If she finds out, she'll be upset."

"I'll be diplomatic."

Ellalyn hadn't mentioned any friends, but she had a coworker who might know more about Ellalyn's life than Ellalyn was willing to reveal. I planned to enjoy a side trip to the Green House of Antiques on a day when Lola would be waiting on customers. If I didn't find any pertinent information, I could always buy myself a new series book.

~ * ~

The next school day went well, considering a heat wave that refused to end, an alarmingly high absentee rate, and a steady stream of students who came down with a sudden illness requiring a trip home, AKA, the ice cream parlor or the beach.

Then came my fifth period American Literature class, and a challenging William Faulkner short story I'd saved for the end of the course— and Rusty Delmar sitting haughtily in his assigned desk, elbow on his textbook, demanding makeup work.

"I don't have it," I said.

"Why not?"

"I'm waiting to hear from your counselor. You realize I can't rewrite an entire course for you. Also, you've missed quizzes and tests and a major research paper, not to mention two American novel reports."

"I can make it all up," he insisted.

"In a week? Not likely. It's too much."

"Give me a chance," he said.

A chance? I wasn't averse to handing out second chances, or even third and fourth chances, but in this case accommodating Rusty was one hundred percent wrong in my estimation.

I wasn't ruining his life. He could always take a summer school course, and he'd have his diploma. Only not the trimmings that went along with a traditional Marston High School graduation. Ceremony, pictures, parties. Especially parties.

The girl who sat in front of Rusty, a petite and chatty little blonde, piped up. "You *have* to let Rusty graduate," she told me.

I ignored her, hoping her voice wasn't the first of many. Sensing that I wouldn't readily grant his request, Rusty had most likely recruited his friends to speak for him.

No teacher likes to be told she has to do something except steer the class back on track, and I didn't need to be told that. I really should have assigned the Faulkner story for earlier in the course when the fall air was crisp and student minds somewhat fresh. Well, next year.

"Everyone, turn to page two hundred and four," I said, noting that Rusty's book was closed, still serving as an armrest.

A hot day, a whiny student, a looming problem, and a story better suited for a college course, I thought. I would have to guide my students slowly through it, wishing I'd had some input into selecting material for this textbook. All I had was my love for Southern literature and the desire to share it with my students.

I told myself that I still liked my career choice, but maybe I should have become a librarian.

~ * ~

Later that day, the thought returned when I stepped inside the Foxglove Corners Public Library. This was an oasis indeed, nicely cooled, and blessedly quiet. Hardly anyone spoke above a whisper, no papers littered the floor, and the shelves held a treasure trove of books to transport the avid reader to other worlds.

Well, I'd made my decision a long time ago, and perhaps working in a library had a downside. At the moment, though, I couldn't think of one.

Miss Eidt sat at her desk perusing a catalog. Dressed in a pale peach suit with a double strand of pearls, she appeared to grow younger and happier with each passing day. Her silvery hair had a luminous shine enhanced by the diamond engagement ring on her finger as she moved her hand languidly in front of her face. Before long, we would be planning her wedding.

Blackberry, the once-feral cat, leaped down to the floor and fled toward the shadows between the stacks. Miss Eidt set the catalog to one side.

"How nice to see you on a school day, Jennet," she said.

"I'm in the mood for a little light reading," I said. "Anything but William Faulkner. Are there any new books in the Gothic Nook?"

She smiled. "Nothing new, but we added a boxful of old Gothics."

"That," I said, "is exactly what I need. School has been grueling."

"Are you going to take a vacation this summer?" she asked.

"A staycation as usual, but I have a new mystery to solve. That'll keep me busy."

I told her about Rainbow's disappearance. Usually, she was excited to hear about a new mystery in Foxglove Corners, ready to offer her help and the resources of the library. But when I finished my tale, I noticed that the anticipated excitement wasn't forthcoming. She looked serious. Even worried.

"What is it?" I asked.

"You say the dog went missing in Woodsboro Park?"

"Yes, last Saturday during a collie event."

"I didn't think it would ever happen again. At least I hoped it wouldn't. Oh, Jennet, I'm so afraid the collie will never be found."

Eight

"The summer of 2001," Miss Eidt said. "I remember that time like it was yesterday."

We sat in her office waiting for the teakettle to whistle. She lifted the top of the cookie jar, a white cat with a glittery red bow on its head.

"Pineapple drop cookies," she said. "I made them this morning. Just the thought of that horrible place makes me feel ill. I need a jolt of sugar."

"What happened?" I asked.

"A little girl named Celia Loring vanished during an outing in the park. Into the thin air, they said. For months, it was all anybody could talk about. To this day, no one knows what became of her. I kept every article. Let's see…"

She opened the middle drawer of a file cabinet and rifled through the neatly labeled pastel folders stored inside. Some of them were so thin they might be empty. Others practically overflowed with clippings.

"It happened in August. That was such a hot summer. Joanne blamed it on the heat. Well, on the heat and herself."

"Who was Joanne?" I asked.

"Celia's aunt, Joanne Linder. Celia was spending the weekend with her."

The teakettle shrilled. I brewed our tea while Miss Eidt searched through the contents of a yellow folder, 'Local Disappearances—Twenty First Century.' She handled each clipping with extreme care, as if it were a rare artifact that would crumble to dust.

"Here we are."

She arranged eight articles on the table in front of me. Like much of the material in Miss Eidt's outmoded vertical file, the paper had a yellowish cast. The longest story included a slightly grainy picture of Celia. She had long blonde hair with bangs and a shy half-smile.

Miss Eidt said, "It was close to ninety degrees and humid that day. Joanne had packed a lunch, and they went to Woodsboro Park so Celia could play on the swings and slides. There were maybe two dozen boys and girls there that day, some adults chaperoning the kids, and a couple of people walking their dogs.

"Joanne sat on a bench watching the kids play while she ate her sandwich. She looked away for a few minutes, and when she looked again, she didn't see Celia with the others."

The story was hauntingly similar to the theft of Rainbow. Ellalyn had kept her eyes on her precious black collie until a friend drew her into a brief conversation. In that brief time of inattention, Rainbow was gone.

Disappeared.

"At first, Joanne thought Celia might have wandered away from her friends," Miss Eidt said. "She liked to chase butterflies. She might have seen an especially pretty one."

"Woodsboro Park must have been smaller in those days," I said.

"It was. The extra property and the woods came later with the Browning legacy. In those days, there was a fountain in the park. People threw coins in the water and made wishes."

"I don't remember seeing a fountain," I said.

Miss Eidt sighed. "There's another sad story. It was taken apart. About five years after Celia vanished, a little boy drowned in it. They say he was reaching for coins, lost his balance, and fell in."

"And no one saw him?"

"Apparently not. It doesn't take long for someone to drown."

"Good grief. Woodsboro Park sounds positively lethal."

"So it would seem, but over time, the stories have been forgotten."

I sat back, nibbled on my cookie, and thought about Celia's vanishing. A hot day. Children stirring up the air as they swung to and fro while the sun beat down on the park and from somewhere came the happy sounds of a summertime tune. A passing ice cream truck...

Wait. Who said anything about an ice cream truck?

Well, there might have been one. The ice cream truck was a traditional part of the summer picture.

How strange that nobody saw those things happen. It was as if at certain times a malignant mist descended on the park, providing cover for unthinkable happenings.

But Miss Eidt was talking. I didn't want to miss a single detail.

"Joanne covered every inch of that park. People helped her. She called the police, and they interviewed all the other children and the few adults who were still there. All to no avail. Celia was gone. They never found her. Or her body."

"Someone must have lured her away," I said. "But you'd think the other kids would have noticed when suddenly Celia wasn't there."

"Apparently, they didn't.

And five years later, nobody saw a little boy lean over a fountain's basin, hoping to pull coins out of the water? Nobody heard his cry?

I could picture the scene. Children excited to be in the park, running, yelling, completely absorbed in their own activities, as were the adults.

The tale Miss Eidt told was chilling and somehow wrong. Something was missing. But what? I gathered the clippings into a neat stack. I would read them later. Miss Eidt wasn't finished talking.

"Joanne stayed in the park until dark," she said. "She went over every inch of the ground. multiple times. Later, she said she felt Celia was still in the park, somewhere. Where else could she be?"

"Gone," I said. "You sound as if you were there that day."

"I wasn't, but like everyone else, I heard about Celia's disappearance on the news. I recognized the name of Celia's aunt. Joanne Linder and I graduated from high school together. I didn't know her well until

Celia vanished. I called on her then and, after that, she used to visit me frequently. We became friends.

"Joanne talked about that day over and over again. She blamed herself. After all, Celia was in her care. And like I said, she blamed the heat. If they hadn't gone to the park that day...if they'd gone to a movie instead...or stayed home. If she'd kept her eyes on Celia. For Joanne and Celia's mom, the worst was never knowing."

"What a sad story," I said. "But how can it have any connection to Rainbow's theft?"

Miss Eidt drank the last of her tea. "Probably there's no connection. Celia vanished years ago."

"Woodsboro park is different now," I pointed out. "It's much larger. There are woods and a lake..."

Woods to conceal a heinous deed, a water source to claim another victim.

"It's still the same place," Miss Eidt said. "The same ground. I'm not superstitious, not really, but I think there's something evil about Woodsboro Park. Lucy Hazen would say it was cursed."

Our friend, Lucy Hazen, Foxglove Corner's renowned writer of horror stories for young readers, had an enviable ability to peer into the future and (sometimes) see things yet to happen. I wonder if she knew about the dark side of Woodsboro Park.

Unfortunately, to my knowledge, Lucy couldn't look into the past.

Miss Eidt returned the yellow folder to the file and gathered the Celia Loring clippings for me in a manila envelope. "I hope you find the missing dog, Jennet," she said. "But I won't be surprised if you don't."

Nine

I slipped the envelope into my shoulder bag and rinsed out our teacups. Celia's story had forced me to see the park in a new and sinister way, and I was eager to read the articles for myself. Miss Eidt might have missed an important detail.

"Were there any other horror stories associated with Woodsboro Park?" I asked. "Incidents that didn't attract the attention of the media?"

"None that I know of," Miss Eidt said, "but now we can add the disappearance of the collie."

"I'm going to hope that Rainbow's story has a happy ending. I'll do everything possible to see that it does."

"How can I help?" she wanted to know.

"Could you post a flyer in the library in a prominent place?"

"Will my desk do? Everyone who takes out a book will see it."

"Perfect. I'll drop one off tomorrow. You can bring the reward to their attention. It's a generous one."

Before leaving, I paid a brief visit to the Gothic Nook where vintage chairs and elegant Tiffany style lamps invited the reader to sample the best of the Gothic, ranging from classics like *The Castle of Otranto* to time-worn novels dating from the nineteen sixties and seventies, most of them rescued from estate sales and used bookstores.

I preferred my evil contained between covers that depicted mysterious houses and damsels in distress running toward or away from them. Fictitious evil was by far easier to handle than the real kind, and almost always you could count on a satisfactory solution.

As I gathered a handful of paperbacks by Velda Johnston, I wondered if in volunteering to help Ellalyn find her stolen collie I had embarked on a Gothic-inspired quest. I didn't agree with Miss Eidt's assessment that Woodsboro Park was evil. Disappearances and accidental deaths happened anywhere, at any time.

The park had been in existence for decades. Over the years, countless people had sought relief from the summer heat under its shade trees. Children still played on the slides and swings, enterprising souls still ate their sandwiches and fruit on the aged benches, and usually everyone went home in one piece. Even the kids who had accompanied their parents and collies to the Walkabout last Saturday.

Watch your children, I wished I'd said. *It doesn't take long for a child to drown or a monster to steal one you love.*

But as appalling as those incidents were, they were buried in the past and all but forgotten. Finding Rainbow was my primary concern. Tomorrow was Saturday, which meant I had plenty of time to talk to Lola or Ms. Zara, the new co-owner of the Green House of Antiques. With luck, I would learn something helpful.

~ * ~

The sun sent its rays pounding down on my head and bare arms as I strolled along the street known as Antique Row. It was warm and so humid that even taking a deep breath required an effort. Late May was too early for dog day weather. I'd been wise to drive into Lakeville before the heat of the day discouraged me.

As always, I stopped to admire the window of the Green House of Antiques. Decorated for Easter the last time I'd come this way, it had undergone a sea change. Beach towels and lawn chairs were arranged haphazardly on a drift of faux sand. A backdrop of cloudless blue sky contained a bright orange-red sun.

Antique dolls wore old-fashioned beach attire made to accommodate their size, and the books scattered on the make-believe sand invoked visions of the sea: *The Bobbsey Twins at the Seashore, Beverly Gray on a World Cruise, Robinson Crusoe, The Spirit of Fog Island.*

Seashell wind chimes announced my arrival as I opened the door and stepped into a high wave of cool air. Immediately, soft music engulfed me, muted strains that conjured an image of falling water.

Suddenly, I wished I could take an oceanside vacation. Yes, with eight rough-coated collies panting in the heat. Well, I could dream.

Three young girls had stationed themselves at the jewelry counter where bold winter colors had been replaced by white necklaces with matching earrings and gold chains. Aside from them, I was the only customer.

Lola, whom I hadn't seen at the Green House for a while, was working today wearing a long floaty blue dress and a hat decorated with wildflowers. She set her Starbucks coffee cup on the check-out counter and greeted me.

"Good morning," she said. "How can I help you today?"

"I just came in to browse and cool off," I said.

"We have several new items to make your summer brighter. Like these treasures." She pointed to a set of six enormous bowls shaped like seashells and painted blue and green. They were too gaudy and clunky, not at all to my taste.

"They're perfect for soup or salad," Lola added. "Or perhaps to add a nautical decoration to a seaside cottage."

"I'll just check out the series books," I said. "Will Ellalyn be in later? I was hoping to see her."

"Oh, sorry, no. She's on vacation this week. Can I give her a message?"

Good. The coast was clear.

"I just wanted to tell her how sorry I was about her dog."

Lola picked up her coffee and frowned. "What about her dog?"

"Didn't you know? Rainbow went missing last Saturday at a collie event in Woodsboro Park."

"Oh, no! How could that happen?"

When I told her about the strange substitution of another tricolor collie for Rainbow, she said, "That sounds like one of our mystery stories."

"It's certainly a mystery," I said.

"Ellalyn must be frantic. She loves that dog."

Now what to ask? I should have prepared a list of questions earlier. I wanted to know as much as possible about Ellalyn's background and her friends.

"So...you knew she had a collie?"

"Everybody did," Lola said. "She wore a brooch with Rainbow's picture on it. If anyone admired it, she'd tell them all about her."

Which contradicted Ellalyn's claim that her customers didn't know anything about her life away from the Green House.

Which also meant there might be legions of suspects and possibly an enemy in Ellalyn's life. But how could I find them or even know who they were?

"She had so many stories," Lola was saying. "Like the time Rainbow chewed up two twenty-dollar bills. Ellalyn had to pick up replacements at the bank. Or the way she kept stealing and hiding her slippers. Or the St. Patrick's Day cake she ate...she had green frosting all over her muzzle."

"Puppy stuff," I said, remembering Halley's antics. My other collies had come to me as adults.

"Honestly," Lola said. "Ellalyn was like a new mother. She even had pictures of Rainbow on her phone."

So did I, along with framed snapshots of my own collies throughout the house.

"What happened to the other dog, the one left in her place?" Lola asked.

The changeling collie. That was a good question and, possibly, a lead I hadn't seriously considered.

"She's in Rescue," I said. "Sue Appleton will find a home for her if her owner doesn't show up."

Of course, if he did, we'd most likely have our thief.

The girls had made their selections. Lola excused herself to ring up their purchases, and I strolled through the store, searching for additions to my series collection and planning another stop—at Sue Appleton's ranch.

Ten

I took my sole purchase, *The Dark Beneath the Pines*, an old hardcover Gothic by Anne Eliot that I chose because the title conjured visions of shadowy, cool woods—and ventured back outside, taking the first few steps under a burning sun.

Good grief, it was hot for mid-morning. I felt as if my makeup were melting, and that I had been wearing my blue shirtwaist for twenty-four hours. The material wasn't supposed to wrinkle, but the dress looked like a garment that had been too long in the dryer.

I shied away from my reflection in a shop window.

By the time I reached my car, I had convinced myself that only a lime cooler at Clovers would restore my flagging energy.

I unlocked the door and stepped quickly back from the onslaught of heat trapped in the interior. The upholstery was steaming, and the steering wheel felt like a firebrand. I sat inside with the door open for a few minutes, trying to summon a modicum of enthusiasm for the gargantuan task I'd set myself. Then I turned on the air-conditioning. There. Much better.

You don't have to do it alone," I told myself, and set a course for Clovers, hoping Annica was working.

~ * ~

Driving down lonely country roads with never a vehicle or runner in sight gave me ample time to think. Lola's information, while welcome, only emphasized the unlikelihood of my finding the person who had subjected Ellalyn to such a cruel prank.

I reminded myself that it wasn't a prank, but a cleverly thought-out attempt to hurt Ellalyn by the enemy she didn't think she had.

For a moment, I wished I hadn't offered to help her find Rainbow, because it seemed this was one mystery I wouldn't be able to solve. The impossible one. Celia Loring had vanished, never to be seen again. Had Rainbow met the same fate? Would Woodsboro Park keep its secrets?

"You're the detective," Brent had said.

I didn't feel like one. Certainly I didn't have the necessary qualifications. I was an English teacher. On the other hand, I also rescued collies, and Rainbow was a collie in distress.

I reviewed the little I knew. So far, no one had come forward to collect the reward. Ellalyn had claimed her customers were unaware of her private life, a fact which Lola's observations contradicted. I'd have to talk to Ellalyn again, to encourage her to look more deeply into her associates.

But what if she were prevaricating? No, that made no sense. Everything about this case was puzzling.

~ * ~

Annica was busy filling the dessert carousel with strawberry tarts and cupcakes, looking sunny but crisp and cool in a yellow sheath and earrings shaped like miniature daisies. No wrinkled garments for her.

"Good morning," I said. "You're always keeping the carousel full."

"I have to. The muffins and doughnuts are all gone. Our desserts go flying off the shelves. We have strawberry pies today. Anyway, this is my favorite place in the restaurant."

Mmm. All I'd come for was a lime cooler, but all right. A piece of strawberry pie sounded good.

"Is there any word about Rainbow yet?" she asked as I seated myself in the booth I considered mine.

"She's still missing."

"Lots of our customers have asked me about the reward," she said. "It's a powerful motivator."

"I hope."

"What can *we* do? *Now*?"

"I think we've done it all. When school's out, I'd like to take a road trip to Maple Falls to talk to Rainbow's breeder," I said. "I hope you can come with me."

"I'll plan on it. But why?"

"What if this is all about Rainbow?"

"I don't understand."

In truth, neither did I. It was only an idea, still undeveloped, but nonetheless gaining strength. This gorgeous black collie, a cherished pet, desired by some nebulous villain for an as-yet-unfathomable reason.

There's always a reason; it never stays unfathomable.

"I haven't figured it out, yet," I said, "but my first thought was that Rainbow's theft was a strike at Ellalyn. That still could be, but maybe I should look at it from a different perspective."

"You lost me," Annica said. "Can't we do something simple?"

"I've called all the shelters, replaced missing flyers, asked Jill Lodge at the *Banner* to write a follow-up story...Crane keeps an eye out for her when he's on patrol. I don't know what else to do except wait, and that's hardly productive."

"Brent is going to add to the reward—again," Annica said.

"That'll help."

"We'll find her," Annica said.

I smiled. "Promise?"

"Or die trying," she added.

~ * ~

After a quick stop at home to give the dogs an outing and fresh water, I drove to Sue's ranch as none of my collies was inclined to walk. Napping in a cool house a few steps away from their water bowl was more appealing.

Sue's dogs had the same idea. They were outside lying in the shade of the house while Sue weeded her flowerbeds. They all looked my way as I turned into the drive.

"It's too hot for gardening," I said.

Sue brushed an imaginary bit of dirt from her cheek. "I don't stay outside long. A half hour is my limit."

"At that rate, you'll never get rid of all the weeds."

"I'm just trying to make the house look presentable."

I looked for Pepper in the collie mash-up and called her name. She stretched and padded toward me, tail a-wag. Bluebell followed her. I gave both dogs light pats on the head. It was too hot for anything more vigorous.

Sue leaned her trowel on a box of weeds. "She remembers you."

"Maybe." The little black collie was most likely looking for the person who had abandoned her in another dog's crate.

"Let's sit on the porch," Sue said, apparently happy to abandon her chore.

"How is Pepper doing?" I asked.

"Adjusting well after a few unhappy days. She's so smart, Jennet. Someone trained her well. She knows what I want before I say anything. I'm going to keep her," she added. "Well, naturally I couldn't place her without knowing if her owner is out there somewhere."

We settled ourselves in wicker chairs, and Sue took a bottle of water from a cooler.

"That doesn't seem likely," I said. "At one time, I thought the thief just grabbed a dog who resembled Rainbow."

"Not that tricolor collies are rare, but one of the right age and sex might not be so easily acquired if needed in a hurry. It doesn't look like anybody is looking for Pepper."

"Everything about this suggests meticulous planning," I said.

"What are we going to do about Rainbow?" she asked.

I lifted the water to my mouth. It was only moderately cool, but better than nothing.

"The whole affair is getting pretty complicated," I said. "We have Ellalyn's collie to find, along with Pepper's owner and the person who's caused all this turmoil. It's like Rainbow vanished into thin air, but that only happens in a Lucy Hazen novel."

Or Foxglove Corners.

"I'm having second thoughts about Ellalyn Zoller," I said. "I don't know if she's confused, devious, or just oblivious."

"You don't think she's lying about losing Rainbow, do you?"

"Not at all. People saw her in the crate...then she was gone. At the moment, I don't know what to think except that strange things have happened in Woodsboro Park."

And maybe that was the answer.

Eleven

That night I had a weird dream. Fragments of it hovered over my bed, refusing to dissipate even when I was fully awake, the edge of the sheet crushed in my hand. My throat and chest felt damp, and my mind was spinning, recreating the horror that had seemed so real. Just minutes ago.

I was in Woodsboro Park, gliding over ground grown thick with weeds, following a sound of falling water.

There was a path of sorts, dark and narrow, winding its way through tall, twisted trees. Their leaves formed a canopy overhead and stole the light, but it was blessedly cool. Out there, beyond the woods, a relentless sun beat down on the earth.

Strangely, I was carrying Anne Elliot's book, The Dark Beneath the Pines.

The water sound grew louder as I advanced through the woods. At some point, it changed into a voice, barely heard, but definitely there, soft and enticing. A mermaid's call.

I pushed through a stand of tall, prickly bushes and saw the fountain, miraculously brought back to life. Because hadn't it been demolished years ago, destroyed and forgotten, punished for taking a life? The statue, a reclining mermaid, spilled water from an enormous seashell into an oval base.

The splashing sound was so loud it caused a throbbing pain in my ears, and spray fell on my face. But I couldn't back away. The fountain wouldn't allow it.

"Look!" it cried. "Look what I have."

A pot filled with gold coins. Mine for the taking!

Intending to scoop up a handful of gold, I leaned over the rim and peered into the water.

At the bottom of the fountain, a dog lay on her side.

So still. So dead.

Rainbow.

I heard the soft pattering of paws on the floor and heavy breathing. Halley? More likely Misty, who always seemed to know when I needed her, and, at the moment, with the nightmare so fresh in my mind, I needed a dog's comfort. What a horrible dream! It seemed as if I could still see Rainbow stretched out on her concrete grave beneath the water.

We would never find her. Not alive.

Misty whimpered softly and lay her head on the edge of the bed. I let my hand rest on her soft fur, let the vision of Rainbow slowly fade away under a blanket of gold, and soon slept again.

~ * ~

Morning sunlight has the power to erase the most appalling of nightmare images.

I set a platter stacked high with blueberry pancakes in front of Crane, who was breaking strips of bacon into tiny pieces for the beggar-collies. I had long since learned to microwave extra strips.

Never hesitate to spoil your dogs. One day they'll be gone.

I gave the thought a vigorous shove. That wouldn't be today, nor any time soon.

It was going to be a beautiful Sunday, warm and sunny. If only Crane could stay home with me. As soon as he finished his breakfast, he would be gone, the county having a prior claim on his time.

"What are you going to do today, honey?" he asked.

I poured more syrup on my pancakes. "It's so nice out, I think I'll drive up to Woodsboro Park."

I hadn't meant to say that. The only plan I'd made was to write another, more detailed review for my American Lit class. It must be the dream, unwilling to release its hold on me.

Had they really torn the fountain down?

They must have, so long ago that few people remembered it had been a beloved feature of the park. Until the drowning.

"If Annica is free for a drive," I added. "I don't want to go alone."

"Why do you want to go back to the park?" Crane asked.

"To revisit the scene of the crime," I said.

"The collie won't be there."

"I know. I'd just like to..."

What?

"Have a clearer picture of where it happened," I said. "Maybe I can figure out how somebody spirited Rainbow out of the park without being seen."

"Just be careful," Crane said.

Catching a glimpse of Candy's tail disappearing under the table and an empty space on Crane's plate, I passed him the platter of bacon.

"Of what?" I asked. "The worst already happened. The thief is long gone."

"But you think the park is...what was the word you used? Sinister?"

"Oh, that was just a feeling."

"Be careful anyway. That's an order. And stay out of the woods."

And watch out for witches! Of course, I didn't say that aloud.

~ * ~

Two hours later, Crane was somewhere in Foxglove Corners patrolling its roads and by-roads, and Annica and I were approaching Woodsboro Park. Misty sat in the back, her eyes on the rapidly passing scenery.

"It's a great day to be going somewhere for a drive," Annica said. "But what do we hope to accomplish?"

She might have been talking to Crane.

"We've reached an impasse. I'd like to go back to the beginning, when we first knew that Rainbow was missing. To start again."

"To see what the Park can tell us?"

Strange how we had begun to think of Woodsboro Park as if it were a character, a key player in the grim drama.

"That sounds like something Lucy Hazen would say," I said.

"We should ask Lucy for her help," Annica said. "Maybe she can look into her crystal ball and tell us where Rainbow is."

I took my eyes off the road for a second and glanced at her. "Lucy's talents don't work that way. Besides, I don't think she has a crystal ball."

"I was just kidding," Annica said. "But we need all the help we can get."

"Agreed."

We have Misty, I thought. *My psychic collie.*

Misty had been at the park when Rainbow disappeared. She hadn't alerted us to danger, but then she wasn't Lassie. Chances are Rainbow's abductor hadn't given off any evil vibes.

I was expecting too much of Misty.

As we entered the park, she scrambled across the back seat to check out the view from the other side of the car. Trees, rolling ground, the requisite swings and slides, children. A crowded parking lot. Why had I imagined we'd have the park to ourselves?

Well, it was Sunday, and the weather couldn't be more perfect for an outing.

"So many people," I said. "I wonder if any of them were at the Collie Walkabout."

Annica reached for the packed lunch she'd brought for us from Clovers. I took Misty's leash and we all walked into the shade of the pines that grew at the entrance.

I didn't know why, but suddenly I had high hopes for our venture.

Twelve

We hadn't taken twenty steps before we were accosted by a little girl with long blonde braids shouting, "Lassie!" She wore a blue sundress that revealed her sunburned arms, an unusual choice of outfit for a day in the park.

Misty, tail wagging, tugged gently on her leash, longing for closer contact with this marvelous little person.

"Can I pet your dog, miss?" she asked.

"Well..."

This rare request gave me pause. I was reluctant to allow an unknown child to touch one of my collies. Suppose Misty inadvertently scratched her or brushed against her arm with her mouth open? Suppose a parent accused my dog of biting the child?

The risk was remote, but a risk it was, and my first and only concern was Misty.

"No, not today," I said.

The child stepped back and tugged on one of her braids, twisting the blue ribbon that glittered in her hair. Clearly, she hadn't expected to be rebuffed.

"You can say hello to her," I added. "It's so hot. Dogs don't like to be handled."

Misty, of course, was busy proving me a liar, sinking into a sit, and raising her paw in true Lassie fashion.

"Why doesn't she have any more color in her fur?" the little girl asked.

"She's a white collie with black and tan head markings," I said. "Like a ghost."

Beside me, Annica hid her laughter with a discreet cough.

"She's the color she's supposed to be," I said. "Her name is Misty."

Annica leaped into the conversation. "What's *your* name, honey?"

"Kristie," she said. "Kristie and Misty." She giggled. "Where can I get a dog like that?"

A dog like Misty? My precious psychic collie was one of a kind, but I imagined any bouncing ball of Lassie fluff would do for this young admirer of the breed.

Misty gave a soft impatient whine and a gentle tug on her leash.

"Are you here with your mom, Kristie?" I asked.

"Naah. I can come alone. I just live over there." She pointed to the south where I couldn't see a single house. Nothing but trees and bushes.

"Okay, Kristie. Well..."

"Our lunch is getting warm." Annica indicated the Clovers bag that contained the sandwiches and cookies she'd packed this morning.

"Bye, Misty." Without a word to us, Kristie scampered off toward the swings, her braids flopping on either side of her small head.

"Meany," Annica said. "Didn't you ever want to pet somebody else's dog?"

"All the time. Whenever I saw one. But you can't be too careful nowadays. Everybody's ready to sue at the least provocation. We don't know that kid or her parents."

"Collies always get the lion's share of attention," Annica said.

"That goes hand in glove with parading one in a crowd."

She waved the Clovers bag in front of me. "I wasn't kidding about these sandwiches getting hot. I see a free bench over there. Let's grab it."

We did and found ourselves close enough to the swings to hear every scream and challenge, every happy cry. I half wished I could have a turn on a swing myself.

Annica began pulling sandwiches out of the bag. "I made ham salad," she said, "and we have brownies. The pop is going to be warm, though. I should have brought the cooler."

I didn't see Kristie but forgot about her as a man sauntered into view leading a blue merle Sheltie on a long lead. The man was strikingly handsome with dark hair, a blue checked shirt, and Levi's. A cowboy type.

I couldn't help staring at him. He would be at home on the cover of a romance novel, hardly the kind of man you would expect to find in real life.

The dog was handsome, too, with showy markings similar to those of my collie, Sky. You don't see a dog with a blue merle coat every day.

But even a dog lover would glance once at the dog and twice at the man. If she were a woman, that is.

Wait! Whoa! What are you doing, admiring another man when you're married and completely in love with the most handsome man in Foxglove Corners?

Misty gave a welcoming bark. The sheltie looked her way but didn't appear to be interested in making her acquaintance. How undoglike.

Annica looked up from her sandwiches. "What a gorgeous—dog."

"Hush. He'll hear you."

Abruptly, the man changed his direction. He was walking toward us.

"Nice collie," he said, extending his palm for Misty to sniff.

His eyes were a clear shade of blue with an entrancing gleam. You might say a wicked gleam. Definitely cover model material.

"What's your dog's name?" Annica asked.

"This is Angus. I found him in the park about a week ago. I'm still looking for his owner."

"That's strange," I said. "A dog disappeared from here last week. A rough collie."

"Oh, at that big collie walk. I heard about it."

"We're helping her owner find her," I said.

"Any luck?"

"Not yet."

"And I can't find this one's owner. I figured he brought Angus to the park. Then...I don't know. Maybe Angus got away from him."

"How did you know the dog's name?" Annica asked.

"He was wearing a collar with a name tag attached but no license."

"Maybe he was abandoned," I said.

"Could be. If I don't find his owner, I'll keep him. Are you ready, boy?"

Angus rose from his sit and glanced at the blue-eyed stranger. Yes, stranger. We hadn't introduced ourselves. Now it was too late, or rather it would be awkward.

"Enjoy the afternoon, ladies and collie," he said and led Angus away.

When he was out of earshot, Annica said, "I should have asked him what *his* name was."

Ah, Brent, I thought. *You'd better quit procrastinating.*

"Woodsboro Park has the best scenery in Foxglove Corners," she said. "But let's get back to work."

She handed me a sandwich which wasn't as warm as she'd feared. Actually, with crisp lettuce and Mary Jeanne's homemade white bread, it tasted almost as fresh as if it had just been assembled.

"Rainbow's crate was just beyond the entrance," Annica said. "Maybe thirty yards? Whoever made the exchange would have spirited her out that way, I think. People were coming in with their collies, and some were leaving. It would have been congested. Who would notice one rough collie being led out to the lot?"

"That's pure speculation," I said. "He could also have taken Rainbow through the woods, maybe to the lake. He might have had a getaway car waiting. Anyway, what we need to know is who did this. And why. Look around. Do you recognize anyone from the Walkabout?"

"Not really. All I see are kids. There were mostly adults here last week."

She was right. Without an event scheduled, the park belonged to the regulars again. Children of all ages were enjoying the swings and slides or just tearing around and screaming.

As I unwrapped a brownie, I looked again for the little girl with the braids who had wanted to pet Misty but didn't see her. All the girls in my view had short or shoulder-length hair and wore casual outfits. There wasn't a sundress in sight.

Where could Kristie have gone?

Thirteen

Licking her chops, Misty eyed my brownie. I gave her another one of her own treats, which seemed to satisfy her, and turned back to the scene that was playing out in front of me.

There were perhaps a dozen children in constant motion, the bright colors of their clothing blending together to form a kaleidoscopic montage. Nowhere did I see a girl with braids in a blue sundress. Certainly she would stand out in this crowd.

"Do you see Kristie?" I asked.

Annica shook her head. "She's probably sulking. You hurt her feelings when you wouldn't let her pet Misty."

"Maybe."

But I didn't think Kristie had taken my rebuff to heart as she'd gone on to ask questions about Misty's coloration.

As I looked again at the children congregating around the play equipment, a strange thought tugged at me. An impossible thought. But could it be?

"Kristie didn't resemble the other little girls," I said.

"No, she looked like a refugee from a dress-up birthday party."

"She said she lived that way." I pointed south. "What's on the other side of the park?"

"Probably empty land. We'll check it out when we leave."

"She was here alone," I pointed out.

"Right. But I don't see any adults around. Just kids."

"Kids who don't really need supervision unless they're very young," I added, remembering the boy who had met his death in the fountain. Surely someone should have been watching him. "It's a large park, and there's the lake..."

And woods, all part of the park's recent acquisition. Dark close-growing trees with grasping branches and roots that could rear out of the ground. Like snakes. Nightmare stuff. And don't forget mosquitoes and other noxious forms of wildlife.

"Kristie may have gone exploring in the woods. They can be dangerous."

"Alone? You're giving your imagination free rein again," Annica said.

"That isn't necessarily a bad thing."

"Not if you remember to rein it in."

She was right. We had come to Woodsboro Park ostensibly to find a clue to Rainbow's disappearance. Nonetheless, my thoughts insisted on drifting back to Celia Loring and the old mystery. The facts I knew formed themselves into a possible scenario.

Celia's aunt eating her lunch, maybe on this very bench, and thinking how about how sweet the plum was. Concerned about juice dripping on her blouse. Searching in her bag for a tissue.

Celia slipping away from the swings, moving gracefully with an enticing breeze.

Enter a diversion...maybe a gorgeous butterfly, an unexpected sighting of a wild rabbit, a running puppy, anything really...and she was gone, skimming across the uneven ground in pursuit. It would only take a few seconds for her to vanish from sight. From the earth.

A second's inactivity to everlasting regret. Did it happen that way?

A flash of bright color burst into my re-creation, and I focused on the here and now. A woman all in orange—slacks and low-cut tank top—bore down on the children, brandishing a popsicle—yes, orange—as if it were a knife.

"Hey, Cindy. Time to come home."

"Aw, Mom..." The little girl attired in a peach outfit kept swinging. "Ten more minutes?"

"Now! March!"

Cindy brought the swing to a stop but stayed in the seat.

"Dogs and kids," Annica said with a smile. "Just try to get them out of the park."

Cindy's mother grabbed her daughter's arm, not gently, and yanked her to her feet.

"There's something about that woman," I said. "Now, where did I see her?"

Then I caught the memory before it could flit away. Here. It was here!

"She was in the park last week," I said. "Standing just behind Ellalyn, after Rainbow vanished."

"How can you be sure?" Annica asked.

"She was wearing her sunglasses pushed up in her hair. She wasn't saying anything, not offering to help. Just standing there, watching."

"Well, so were we, and a lot of people. Now she's walking away."

So she was, one hand on Cindy's arm, the other holding the popsicle. Cindy was whining, but I couldn't hear what she was saying. The woman was silent, determined, moving quickly.

Misty, who had been snoozing at my feet, snapped to attention, ears tipped. A disturbance of any kind, especially if it involved a young person, made her nervous.

I stroked her head. "It's all right."

I think.

"Okay," Annica said. "You have a new talent. A photographic memory. But just because that woman was at the Collie Walkabout doesn't mean she was involved in Rainbow's disappearance."

"No."

But I was desperate for a clue. Any clue. Unfortunately, this, the orange one, was most likely already out of the park and my life. Of course, logic told me that if she had just snatched another person's collie at the Walkabout, she wouldn't be staying around to witness the aftermath. And where would she have stashed Rainbow?

I gathered the remains of our lunch and looked for a trash receptacle. Perhaps it was time for us to leave, too. The sun was hotter than it had been only an hour ago, and the brownie had made me thirsty for lemonade or a lime cooler or even a tall glass of water crammed with ice cubes.

Misty gave a soft 'I want water, too' whimper. Sometimes I thought she could read my mind. But I should know better. Of course, she needed water.

I gave her a drink from the bottle I'd brought for her and rose, tightening my hand on her leash.

A snatch of tinny musical notes carried on the breeze caught my attention. Delicate, happy, fairy notes. A familiar melody:

All around the mulberry bush
The monkey chased the weasel
The monkey thought 'twas all in fun
Pop! goes the weasel.

The ice cream truck's siren's call. Frosty sweet treats. Thirty-one flavors!

Strangely, there wasn't a rush of children's feet to answer it. On the contrary. A hush fell over the park. Annica held a compact up to her face. She checked her lipstick, then twisted a red-gold curl around her finger.

Misty tilted her head again, her gaze fastened on the woods.

"An ice cream truck," I said.

Annica slipped her compact back into her tote bag. "Where do you see an ice cream truck?"

Fourteen

"Don't you hear the music?" I asked. "All around the mulberry bush?"

"No, and I hate that song. A little animal getting squished. Blood and guts. Ugh."

I'd never thought about it that way. But many nursery songs were unabashedly violent. Take *Three Blind Mice* and *Humpty Dumpty*.

"It has a catchy melody, though," I said.

It had. I didn't hear it now.

I stared into the woods. Deep dark woods. The screams of children having a good time filled the air. Misty began to pant. Her sweet collie face bore a worried expression. I didn't hear the musical notes or see anything remotely resembling an ice cream truck.

"I may have imagined it," I said. "I have my mind on a soda fountain."

"Think, Jennet. A truck would hardly go trundling through a park."

Misty heard it, I told myself. *But let it go. There's nothing to hear now.*

"It must have been passing out on the road," I said.

71

"It's all country around the park, but there's a new development not too far away, Woodsboro Estates. I'll bet that's where that sheltie's cute owner lives."

"Don't you mean that cute sheltie's owner?" I asked.

"Uh, no." She winked. "The adjective's in the right place."

I dropped our lunch bag, by now empty except for one crumbled gravy bone, into the nearest trash receptacle.

"I'm getting a sunburn," Annica said. "My nose is turning red."

I gave Misty the bone. "This wasn't the best idea, I guess, but I feel that Woodsboro Park is the heart of the mystery."

Both of them, I added to myself. An enormous piece of the woods fitted out with juvenile instruments of pleasure. A dark and dangerous place, currently overcast but still warm. A place of secrets. But not impenetrable.

Annica said, "Did you read where they're going to build a gazebo somewhere on the new land?"

"That should make the woods less isolated."

And that would be good for a place that attracted so many children.

"The mystery won't solve itself," I said. "We can't afford to waste time. I'm going to see Ellalyn as soon as possible. Maybe something's happening behind the scenes."

Every day that passed, Rainbow moved further away. Would she soon be beyond our power to reclaim her?

Not if we hurry.

~ * ~

Ellalyn was impossible to get hold of. Anyone would think she wasn't eager for updates about her stolen dog. Or that she had given up. I left her three voice messages and decided to wait for her to respond.

I knew where to find her, of course, and stopping at the Green House of Antiques would be no hardship. But I was suddenly out of time. The weekend was over. School loomed, and the last days promised to be hectic.

That proved to be an understatement. A carnival atmosphere had descended on Marston High School. Attendance was sporadic, clothing was ultra-casual and, in some cases, neon bright, and noise ruled the halls. Chaos mixing with jubilation. The end was in sight, and the warm, seductive weather continued.

Embedded in the carnival was a charming oasis-for-faculty-only, the courtyard where Leonora and I could eat our lunch in peace, listen to the fall of water from the fountain, and pretend that we were enjoying a picnic and didn't have three more classes before we could go home to Foxglove Corners.

Today a cloud hovered low in the air, a note from Principal Grimsley. I was instructed to see him in his office during my conference hour.

That couldn't be good.

I unwrapped my sandwich, realizing I wasn't hungry. But I would be by the end of the day. I'd better eat, build strength and resistance. I opened a bottle of water, took a long, satisfying drink, and told Leonora about the note.

"I'll bet it's about your student, Rusty," she said.

"That would be my guess. I don't think he's naming me Teacher of the Year."

The seniors' last day was almost here. The day of reckoning.

"I haven't changed my mind about failing Rusty," I said. "I talked to his counselor. He won't tell her where he spent all those hours when he should have been in American Lit. In fact, he's stopped attending my class."

"But that's good, isn't it?"

"It's suspicious."

That meant no more demands for make-up work. No more pleas from his friends. It was an uneasy peace before the storm.

Did I really think the problem would go away?

"Don't give in to them," Leonora said. "Set a precedent, and it'll happen again, the next time to another teacher."

She handed me a brownie, wrapped in leftover red Christmas plastic. "For courage," she said.

~ * ~

The principal sat at his desk, an unflappable despot in navy blue and white, a mini-American flag pinned to his lapel and his signature smile pasted on. In another man, that smiling countenance would communicate friendliness. In Grimsley, it flashed a different message: *Beware.*

Strength, I thought. *Resistance. Courage.*

"It seems we have a problem," he said.

I waited.

Admit nothing.

"You have a student who claims you're deliberately preventing him from graduating."

"And how am I doing that?"

"By refusing to give him make-up work in a course he needs in order to graduate."

"Are those the only details you have?" I asked.

I was on firm ground, having proof of Rusty's long string of absences in my gradebook, which I guarded with my life.

"Rusty thinks you're confusing him with another student."

I couldn't refrain from smiling. "There's only one boy with red hair in my fifth hour class."

It was Grimsley's turn to wait.

"Here are the facts," I said. "Rusty attended class ten times in January. On two of these occasions, he was tardy. He hasn't turned in a single assignment. Then last week, he reappeared and asked for make-up work. After four months. Naturally, I refused."

"Rusty says you marked him absent when he was there. He claims you're not always careful about taking attendance."

I bristled at that accusation. Good grief! Grimsley sounded as if he believed it.

"You can check the daily absence sheets," I said, thankful that we lived in the computer age.

"He could do some make-up work and take the final exam. If he passes it..."

I couldn't believe Grimsley was saying that, he being such a stickler for school rules, and his favorite phrase being 'time on task.'

"Participation in class discussion is a large part of a student's grade," I reminded him. "My other three seniors are writing research papers in lieu of a test."

I threw out my last argument.

"I'm following the school's policy. A dozen unexcused absences in a class results in a failure."

"Well, then..."

At some point, Grimsley's smile had disappeared. He was obviously unhappy with me. I didn't care.

"Then it's up to you to follow your conscience."

"Yes."

"Just be sure of your facts," he said.

Fifteen

Leonora and I took turns commuting to Marston High School, which was an hour's drive to the south. This was my week to drive. Freeway traffic to Foxglove Corners was light, and the next exit would take us to a little-traveled scenic country road.

By now, I should start to feel a little lighter, the cares that came with teaching at Marston High School having slowly melted away. It wasn't happening. The ten minutes in the principal's office, and his parting words, kept replaying in my mind.

"How can a concession sound like a threat?" I asked, as I steered the car into the right lane.

"Everything Grimsley says has a subtle threat embedded in it," Leonora said. "But don't worry. You have right on your side."

"I do. If Rusty and his kind were allowed to prevail, all we'd need to do is hand out textbooks and packets of assignments. Eliminate the teacher. Everyone passes."

For a moment, I had a chilling notion that I was describing a school of the future. All computers and robo-teachers.

"There *is* something, though," Leonora said. "Something Adam told me in confidence. Grimsley used to change teachers' grades for

77

athletes if they weren't high enough for scholarships. On the sly, of course. That was years ago. But who knows if he still does it? He could change Rusty's grade to a 'C' or 'D' and voila! Rusty could graduate."

Why was I not surprised? Coach Adam Barrett had been Leonora's good friend before her marriage. In the sometimes-twisted world of Marston High School, the athletic department and the administration walked hand in glove through the days. As Adam's friend, Leonora was ideally positioned to hear gossip.

"Who goes back and check past records once the school year is over?" she added. "I know I don't."

"This is different," I said. "Everybody would know if Rusty went through graduation and received his diploma."

"Who's to say he couldn't receive it privately?"

I'd never considered that possibility. I didn't want to.

"What bothers me is Grimsley's interest in this," I said. "Why does he care? Rusty didn't pass a required class. He isn't entitled to graduate. That's a school rule."

If the principal cared, if Rusty's counselor cared, they might have been able to nip his entitled, destructive behavior in the bud months ago.

"Could this interrogation be directed at harassing me?" I wondered aloud.

"We know the principal loves harassing teachers, especially women," Leonora pointed out. "Anyway, soon it won't be an issue."

I had been so engrossed in our conversation, so troubled by this new suspicion, that I was hardly aware of turning off the exit, of heading home with spring-turning leaves on either side of the road. They stirred gently in the wind, reminding us that summer wasn't far behind. I desperately needed a break from the career I loved.

"Rusty's grade stands," I said. "Come what may."

~ * ~

Home. I had fallen in love with the green Victorian farmhouse on Jonquil Lane at first sight, before Crane came along, long before my collie brood grew from one to eight.

My home was a never-failing source of comfort for me, my safe haven from the buffeting winds of life—and school. The collies were waiting to greet me, overjoyed that I hadn't deserted them. We went through this drama every school day.

I distributed pats and bones, poured fresh water, and took them outside. While they played, I admired the daffodils that lined the lane. They were so cheerful, all shades of yellow, and like all flowers, they were fragile and wouldn't last.

Gradually, the scene in Grimsley's office shrank and lost its color, tottered in a moment of black and white, and faded out of existence. Velvet and Misty engaged in a mock battle over a stick, and Halley sniffed at a bit of paper debris blown into my emergent flower bed. Each dog followed her own special pursuit. I took a deep, restorative breath.

Country peace and quiet. Why couldn't some clever scientist figure out how to bottle it?

But alas! Nothing endures forever. The hum of a motor insinuated itself into the silence. Eight collie heads turned toward the sound. The stick fell back to the ground unlamented. In the next instant, a sleek white car with sweeping green fins rounded the curve.

Brent in his vintage Plymouth. Treats from Pluto's Gourmet Pet Shop. Maybe a box of candy or flowers for the house, in other words, for me. Brent always came bearing gifts and, invariably, timed his arrival for the dinner hour.

Stuffed cabbages tonight, I thought quickly. I had plenty of them, and all they needed was a few minutes in the microwave.

He parked and, as expected, brought a bulging shopping bag out of the back seat. Yes, a bag with Pluto's logo. The dogs flocked nosily around him, forgetting their recently returned mistress.

"Hi, Jennet," he said. "I came to give you a progress report on Rainbow."

"Is it good?" I asked.

"Not really."

We went back inside, and he set the Pluto's bag on the counter. Realizing their treats weren't immediately forthcoming, the dogs dispersed to their favorite places in the house, except for Candy and Misty who lay on either side of Brent, their eyes on the hidden treasures currently out of their reach.

"But I've been trying," Brent said. "I heard about a black collie in a Maple Creek shelter. It turned out to be a male. Rainbow is a girl, right?"

I nodded. "Nothing else?"

"Other than that, tricolor collies are in short supply. I hoped increasing the reward would entice the thief to return Rainbow. You wouldn't think she'd be worth that much to whoever took her."

"We don't know why she was taken in the first place," I pointed out. "It may not be a matter of money."

"And we don't know how," Brent said. "I mean, how could anyone spirit her out of the park without attracting attention?"

That didn't entirely puzzle me. The people who had attended the Walkabout would have been focused on their own collies and conversations with their friends. One more person with a black collie would have gone unnoticed.

"Annica and I went back to the park today," I said. "We saw a woman who was there when Ellalyn realized Rainbow was missing. At least I think it was the same woman."

"Did you question her?" he asked.

"No. I only saw her for a few seconds. She came to take her daughter home."

But I should have gone up to her and...done what? Say I was investigating the theft of the tricolor collie who had disappeared last week?

Why not?

All she could do was deny any involvement, and, if by chance she were complicit, she would then be forewarned.

"I hope I'll see her again," I said. "That park is popular with kids."

"I really want to find Rainbow," Brent said. "We promised Ellalyn we'd help her."

"I wonder if Ellalyn is helping herself?"

"Why wouldn't she be?"

I shrugged. "It's a feeling I have. I've left messages for her. She doesn't return my calls. You'd think she'd at least want an update."

I glanced at the clock. Crane would be home soon. I opened a can of root beer for Brent and one for myself. Brent brought out the treats from the Pluto's bag: tarts with some good-for-canines filling. The dogs fell on them.

"I used to think there wasn't a mystery you couldn't solve," Brent said.

"This may be the one."

"We should go back to Woodsboro Park again," he said. "Find that woman, if we can. Look for anyone else who was at the Walkabout and might have noticed something suspicious. We can tack flyers to the trees. Maybe I should keep increasing the reward."

"That's all we can do." I watched the dogs gobble their tarts, two for each one, oblivious of the fate that had claimed one of their own.

"I feel drawn to the park. And it's the last place Rainbow was seen."

"Let's get together and go on a Rainbow hunt, then," he said. "You and me, Annica and Lucy...Lucy might be able to pick up some helpful vibes."

She might at that. Although her special talents didn't quite work that way. But who knew? Besides, I didn't have any other ideas.

The more I thought about that dark, atmospheric, secretive place that had seen more than one tragedy in the past, the more I entertained a disturbing thought.

What if Rainbow had never left the park?

Sixteen

Then there was the cold case of Celia Loring, another victim of Woodsboro Park. Whenever I thought of Rainbow, I remembered Celia's story. She would be grown now, in her mid-twenties, if she were still alive. Which was doubtful.

On the other hand, occasionally I read about missing persons, long believed dead, who resurfaced years later with a variety of explanations, and of dogs who found their way back to their owners against every odd.

Like Lassie Come-Home.

Rainbow, where are you?

I didn't think Rainbow would come home, and, even if she did, she certainly couldn't tell us where she'd been. Meanwhile, school concerns took precedence over my current mystery.

Facing another day of probable angst and conflict, the next morning I dressed in a navy polka dot knit, one of my favorites, and slipped the silver heart locket Crane had given me for Valentine's Day around my neck.

Look good, and you'll have a good day, I told myself.

And I did. No worrisome notes from the principal lurked in my mailbox. My classes were borderline manageable, even my fifth period class. Once again, Rusty was absent.

It was the seniors' last day. I collected their research papers and looked the other way when one of them smuggled pizzas into the room to share with the underclassmen and me.

Grimsley, stay away.

The principal was a tireless defender of the no-food-or-drink in the classroom rule, but according to rumor, he was out of town for two days. Every now and then, it's fun to scrap the day's lesson and just enjoy being a class. Soon, my students would move on and become the stuff of memories. At this point, I knew I'd miss them, even the troublemakers.

I ate my own slice of pizza during my conference period and, for the first time ever, didn't do anything else. And the last bell rang.

"Every day should be like this," Leonora said as we walked to the parking lot, dodging a flotilla of multi-color balloons that sailed through the warm windy air. Flying objects were a harmless way of celebrating school ending and summer vacation beginning.

I wondered if Rusty had abandoned his demand for a free ride to graduation. Somehow, I didn't think he would go quietly.

"It will be, now that the seniors are gone," I said.

Our graduating class had almost a hundred members. Some teachers had entire classes that would disappear. Never fear, though. Grimsley would find other jobs for them.

I reached for a low-flying red balloon, but it escaped. Was that an omen? Mmm. Not unless it burst.

With one more day wrapped up, my thoughts returned to Rainbow.

I unlocked the door. Leonora deposited her books in the back and slid into the passenger's seat.

"Would you mind stopping at the Green House of Antiques with me, or would you rather I drop you off at home?" I asked.

"I'd love to buy myself an end-of-the year present," she said. "We should do something special at the end of every day this week. But why do you want to go to an antique shop?"

"I'm hoping to see Ellalyn. She hasn't returned my calls, and I can't understand why."

Unless somehow she had gotten Rainbow back and neglected to tell us, but I didn't think that was the case. I had the troubling idea that she might have dropped out of sight as completely as her collie. I'd given up the idea of visiting Rainbow's breeder as overkill.

"Let's do it," Leonora said. "I'll check out lamps and jewelry, and you can talk to Ellalyn."

~ * ~

The window of the little shop on the street known as Antique Row was a genuine work of art that changed to reflect different seasons and holidays. It practically invited the passerby to step inside and experience a half hour or more of enchantment.

Today's display still invoked the beach, with a spill of faux sand and a cloudy blue-sky backdrop. Books and antique dolls lounged on rainbow-colored blankets. One mannequin wore an ultra-modest vintage swimsuit.

Leonora gasped. "Who would wear that?"

"Not I. Not even on Halloween."

"Well, no. You'd freeze."

I pushed open the door and silver seashell chimes announced our arrival. We had come at a good time. A few customers browsed quietly in the rows, and a lavender fragrance wafted through the air. I loved this place, loved absorbing the rich old-time ambience and the anticipation of perhaps finding new book for my collection.

A brown-haired girl greeted us with a warm smile. She wore blue jeans and one of the store's frilly vintage blouses with a long string of crystal (or glass) beads. Her name tag—Carly—glittered on the white ruffles.

"Good afternoon," she said. "What can I show you today?"

Leonora hesitated, then said, "I'd like to look at the table lamps."

"And old-time books." I glanced at the half-open door to the back room. "Is Ellalyn working today."

"I'm sorry. Ellalyn isn't with us anymore." Her tone was so serious I thought for an instant that Ellalyn had passed away.

"I thought she was on vacation," I said.

"She was, then she resigned."

"That was sudden."

"I guess. I heard she had a family emergency."

The loss of Rainbow? I wondered. Or something else? Doesn't trouble often come in threes? Perhaps that was why she didn't return my calls. I'd have to get in touch with her in person.

Honestly, this mystery just kept growing.

Leonora and Carly had drifted away to a corner of the shop crowded with antique furniture where authentic Tiffany lamps as well as imitations adorned the tops of graceful side tables. Vintage books, vases, and candlesticks were scattered on all available surfaces.

I wandered down the wavy aisles, idly taking note of titles. There were no Beverly Grays, no Judy Boltons that I didn't already have, and a smudged *Code of the West* by Zane Gray that I examined and replaced.

Nothing reached out to me, and I met Leonora at the register where she was in the process of purchasing an antique brooch.

"They had prettier lamps at Christmastime," she said. "I wanted something with bright jewel colors."

"And I really wanted to talk to Ellalyn. I guess the Rainbow mystery will have to wait."

Seventeen

"Do you think Ellalyn resigned to look for her dog?" Leonora asked as we left the shop.

"Maybe, but working in an antique shop isn't exactly a career. She may have found a better paying job."

Or she might be slowly sinking into a figurative black hole. I couldn't tell. Having her cherished collie stolen was traumatic, but people lose dogs all the time, albeit not under such strange circumstances. Usually, their lives don't come to a standstill. Many continue to grieve quietly and go on with their lives and their jobs.

"It's not like Rainbow died," Leonora said.

"We can't know that. I'm going to reach out to Ellalyn one more time. But not tonight."

"No, we both have schoolwork to do and, like Scarlett said, 'Tomorrow is another day.'"

And what would it bring? Another innocuous school day like today. Maybe something unexpected and wonderful like a break in the Rainbow case.

I could hope.

~ * ~

I knew something was wrong the minute I unlocked my classroom door the following morning. Well, maybe not wrong, but different.

Then I saw the writing...large words printed in white chalk, spaced to cover the entire blackboard: *You'll be sorry!*

Behind me, the noise in the hall faded. I stepped inside, my heart beating faster in the stuffy atmosphere, and stared at the message. The warning. I couldn't take my eyes on those awful words. *You'll be sorry. Why? What was going to happen?*

I had to erase the writing. Quickly. Before my students saw it. I dropped my books on the desk and grabbed the eraser, obliterating one word at a time.

They didn't want to be wiped out of existence. Whoever had written those three words had a heavy hand. I could still see a trace of the letters. I moved the eraser across the board again with more force and over it wrote: 'Review today. All classes.'

Which was what I had planned.

I didn't understand how this could have happened. As always, the custodian had cleaned the room after yesterday's classes, leaving the desks in neat rows and the floor swept. It fairly sparkled in the morning light. Then he would have locked the door; he always did. And he never failed to clean the blackboard.

Either last night or early this morning, someone had entered the room and left those threatening words for me to find.

Someone?

I had no doubt the culprit was Rusty. I refused to give him the credit needed to graduate. I would be sorry.

I had been threatened before in this very room. But these words had shaken me to the core.

I sat at my desk and let my heart resume its normal pattern. I had classes to teach and couldn't let my students know anything had happened. And to think I'd told Leonora we'd have smoother sailing now that the seniors had gone.

After their last day, which was yesterday, they weren't allowed in the building except for graduation practice. But Grimsley was still out of town, and I hadn't seen the hall monitors lately.

Where there's a will there's a way. Anyone could come and go in the school with impunity. And threaten a teacher.

I turned at a shuffle of feet. Megan and Joy, always together and always early.

"Morning, Mrs. Ferguson," Joy said. "Review, huh?" She pulled a compact out of her purse and smiled at her reflection.

"Does that mean no homework?" Megan asked.

"It does, but make sure you've read all the stories. There'll be essay questions on the test."

The bell rang. I glanced at the board, and for a moment my own words seemed to have vanished. In their place, the horrible message reappeared, now written in blood-red chalk. Crimson droplets dripped down to the floor.

~ * ~

"Five more days," Leonora said as we ate lunch in the courtyard. "Then we can blow this popsicle stand. Uh, the school."

"A lot can happen in five days," I said.

I bit into my sandwich. It tasted like sawdust. Not that I'd ever eaten sawdust.

"Really, Jennet," Leonora said. "Threats and curses and the like come with the job. It's not an elementary school where kids give their teachers presents at the end of the year."

I had to smile. "I didn't know they still did that."

"Even I've been verbally attacked on occasion," she added.

I found that hard to believe. Leonora was pretty, vivacious, and popular. She had a connection with her students I could never emulate.

"I hope you're going to report it."

"To Grimsley? I'd rather not."

"To the assistant principal, then. Don't downplay it. Remember the shooting?"

My heart skipped a beat. Instinctively, I reached for my heart locket. My talisman.

I would never forget the student who had opened fire in my classroom or the one who had died.

"I don't regret not giving Rusty a chance to make up practically a whole course worth of work," I said.

"You think it was Rusty?"

"I haven't ruffled any other feathers. That I know of."

"Well, report it to someone. One of the kids has access to a master key. That isn't good."

"You're right."

Even after the shooting in our school, security had been lax, in my opinion. Technically we had three full-time monitors on duty, and teachers whose senior classes had ended had been assigned to patrol the halls.

But were they doing their job or hanging out in the staff lounge drinking coffee?

Which was where I'd be during my conference hour from now on, rather than in my empty room. It only made sense not to isolate myself.

Eighteen

Home. Safe. And as Leonora had said, in five days Marston High School would close for the summer.

But was my home truly safe? I recalled a few dangerous confrontations on my own turf.

All right. Safer, then. Still...

Would the threat possibly follow me to Jonquil Lane? I didn't talk about my home life with my students, but anyone could find my address on the Internet.

I reminded myself that Crane was a deputy sheriff. He had guns. I had eight large dogs and a gun of my own. That I'd never fired it was irrelevant. In any event, my home was definitely safer than my school.

The collies surrounded me, tails wagging, eager for their after-school treats and time outside. Misty claimed the space closest to me, nudging my knee with her long nose and offering comfort, although she didn't know what was wrong.

My psychic collie girl.

After giving the dogs plenty of playtime in the fresh air, I set about preparing dinner. Crane was going to grill hamburgers. My contribution was a pasta salad and dessert. But no matter what I did, the image of the blackboard in my classroom superimposed itself over my random thoughts.

You'll be sorry!

I added a dollop of dressing and gave the salad a vigorous stir. And kept on stirring.

~ * ~

I told my story to an audience of two that evening. Brent had joined us for dinner. In the morning, he planned to drive up north to Maple Falls where a female tricolor collie languished in an overcrowded shelter. Tonight, he spared a thought for my school dilemma.

"Those punks need to be locked up," he said. "In my day, you didn't dare threaten a teacher or even talk back to her."

I smiled. "Where did you go to school, Brent?"

"Saint Barbara's over in Maple Creek."

"Times have changed. Drastically."

"Maybe you should apply for a job at Saint Barbara's, Jennet," Crane said.

Brent hovered over the cheese and crackers tray I'd assembled. "Too late, Sheriff. It's been closed for ten years."

"I'd like to see Jennet teaching in college," Crane added, "or better still, staying home and solving her mysteries."

We'd had this discussion before. I had flirted with the idea of going back to school for a doctor's degree and decided against it.

I said, "It all comes down to balancing the good with the bad, and there's plenty of good at Marston. But darn it! I almost made it to the end of the year without any major drama. I don't know for certain who wrote that warning, but my best guess is Rusty, the kid who wanted credit for not attending a required class."

"How many more days?" Brent asked.

"Five."

"What will you do then?"

"Retire to the country." I smiled at Crane. "Bake Crane's favorite desserts and solve the mystery of Rainbow's disappearance."

I steered the conversation in another direction in the interest of setting vague threats aside, if only for one evening.

"Speaking of mysteries, is the tri at the Maple Falls shelter our only clue?"

"Yes, it isn't going well."

"And I'm not having luck contacting Rainbow's owner. I wonder if she's avoiding me?"

"Why would she do that?" Crane wanted to know. "You're helping her find her dog."

"I haven't done much. Brent is doing it all."

Brent slipped a cube of cheddar to Sky and immediately attracted the attention of the rest of the pack.

"I sure thought it would be easier," he said, scooping up a handful of treats to dispense. "So far there haven't been any takers for my reward."

"Because Rainbow isn't to be found," I said. "I wonder about this collie in the Maple Falls shelter. I don't think it's likely that someone would steal a valuable dog and abandon it."

"Again, it depends on the reason Rainbow was snatched," Brent pointed out. "If only she were microchipped."

We'd learned that, for some reason, Ellalyn had neglected to take that precaution.

"Well, I'm taking her picture along. We'll see if the rescue collie could be our missing girl."

~ * ~

Ellalyn Zoller lived in a picturesque yellow-sided ranch with green shutters and a bay window. A forsythia wreath adorned the door, and a bed of pink petunias circled a Scotch pine in a large front yard island. There was a flagpole attached to the house but no flag. A white picket fence enclosed the back yard.

The house was the embodiment of the American dream. Except the flowers were crying for lack of water, and I didn't see a hose or watering can.

I climbed four steps to the porch. Envelopes and advertisements spilled out of the green mailbox onto the porch and the ground below, an ominous sign.

Either Ellalyn had gone away or she had no interest in collecting her mail, which might indicate depression.

I rang the bell and listened for a sound of footsteps. Nothing. No one. Then I noticed drapes drawn across the windows which, along with unclaimed mail, was a clear welcome signal to burglars.

I rang the bell again, just in case Ellalyn was inside sleeping. If not, perhaps she had extended her vacation or...I really couldn't imagine what she was doing. With Rainbow's fate unknown, why would she keep her distance from people who wanted to help her?

Maybe it was time to withdraw from the search, especially since I didn't know where to turn. But I kept thinking about that fateful day at the park, about Rainbow abducted from her safe crate and spirited away to parts unknown for a reason that eluded me.

I was entitled to be upset with Ellalyn for her silence and apparent disinterest, but not with Rainbow, the beautiful tricolor collie I didn't even know.

For Rainbow's sake, I would resist the impulse to step away from the mystery, even though, at present, it was going nowhere, figuratively frozen in time.

Trying to summon a modicum of enthusiasm, I walked back to my car.

Nineteen

While I was out and about, I decided to stop at the library to visit Miss Eidt and check out a few Gothics for the rapidly approaching summer vacation.

I left the car in the shade of a maple tree and walked to the old white Victorian-turned-library, taking deep breaths of delicious floral-scented air. The flower beds gleamed with freshly watered candytuft and lobelia in shades of blue.

Blue and white. The combination reminded me of Camille's country kitchen, where I always felt so much at home, as I did at the library. I really wanted some new Gothic novels but also wanted to talk to Miss Eidt about Rainbow.

Blackberry, the library's guardian cat, watched me ascend the porch steps from her seat on a white wicker chair. *Her* chair. And don't you forget it. She didn't move, but her bright eyes glittered like precious stones. Anyone would think she was a garden ornament.

"Good kitty," I said, not expecting a response, and pushed open the door.

Dressed in powder blue, one of her favorite colors, Miss Eidt sat at her desk stamping a book, one of a tall stack at her elbow. A beam of light bathed her in a soft glow, turning her hair to silver. As I approached, I noticed that same light beam dancing on her diamond engagement ring.

"I was about to call you, Jennet," she said. "I came across an article that might interest you. It's about Woodsboro Park and mentions Celia Loring. I made a copy for you."

She opened a drawer and rifled through a jumble of papers, eventually finding the one she sought.

"How did we miss it when we were going through the folders the other day?" I asked.

"It's fairly recent, not in the file yet." She handed me the copy. "Last month, a young girl, Sally Holland, disappeared while walking with her friends. Do you know how many kids vanish in Michigan?"

"I have no idea," I said, "but my guess is a lot. There are runaways, children taken by non-custodial parents..."

"Too many. It's like they fall into a black hole."

"Or take a stroll down Huron Court," I added.

Every time I thought about or mentioned that road, a coldness took hold of my heart. Besides being haunted, it had a fragile grasp on time. A traveler on Huron Court could find himself summarily swept away into another season and time. In the blink of an eye, summer showers turned into winter snow flurries. The lucky ones came back.

This didn't always happen. Sometimes Huron Court was simply a country road.

I had personal experience of its anomalies and avoided it as if an evil virus dropped down from every tree that grew along its edge.

"The girls were shopping for prom dresses in Lakeville," Miss Eidt said. "One minute, Sally was there, talking about her date. The next minute, she wasn't. Her friends thought she'd slipped into one of the shops without telling anyone, but that wasn't the case. She vanished. Into thin air, as they say."

"The black hole," I said. "I came in for Gothics, but here's a situation straight from a Victoria Holt novel."

"Except that in a novel, the author has to solve the mystery."

"And in real life we have to do it ourselves."

"In a book, we can usually count on a happy ending," she added.

This was life, however, and, at present, the ending was unknown.

"We have a missing collie," I said, "and maybe now a missing owner. I'll admit I'm baffled."

"You need a good lead, a clue. Something solid to go on."

"I'll read the article now," I said.

The table closest to the paperback carousel was empty. I sat and read and immediately my interest in Woodsboro Park flickered to life, although everybody but Celia Loring had vanished from different places.

The writer cited a number of disappearances in Foxglove Corners, old and new. With today's ready access to the Internet, some of the missing children were quickly found.

And some weren't.

~ * ~

I sat in the same beam of light that had turned Miss Eidt's hair to silver and read the article twice, noting disturbing similarities. The children who had vanished from southeastern Michigan in the past two decades were female with one exception. They ranged in ages from seven to seventeen. Most of them came from stable families and were apparently well-adjusted and happy.

All went missing without a trace, some of them while with friends, none of whom noticed anything amiss. Of the young people profiled in the article, not one was recovered.

Like Celia. Like Rainbow.

Rainbow wasn't a child, of course, but she vanished in mysterious circumstances, like the others.

I slipped the article into my shoulder bag and returned to the desk.

Miss Eidt said, "It's truly frightening, isn't it?"

I nodded. "Where did they go?'

"And who took them?"

I wondered. "Did it start with Celia Loring, or is that just where the writer began his survey?"

"That'll require further research."

"I wish I could talk to Celia's aunt," I said.

"You can."

"How?" I asked.

"She's still alive. I told you we were friends."

So she had. Why had I assumed that the aunt, an eyewitness to Celia's disappearance, was deceased?

"She lives in Maple Creek," Miss Eidt said. "I haven't seen Joanne in ages, but I could call her and set up a meeting. We can visit her together, if you'd like. I'd love to see her again."

"Please do that. I don't know how it could help us find Rainbow, but...well, I'm curious. About Celia—and that park."

Miss Eidt agreed to call Joanne, and I remembered my other reason for coming to the library. No one was currently browsing in the Gothic Nook. I spied a cart loaded with paperbacks waiting to be shelved and headed toward it.

Why was I looking for Gothic novels to read when I was practically living one?

Suddenly I thought of Molly and Jennifer, my two young friends who lived on Sagramore Lake Road and often walked the collie Ginger up and down the roads of Foxglove Corners. What if one day they disappeared?

I could imagine the breaking news: *Girls Vanish While Walking Dog.*

Don't be melodramatic, I told myself.

It probably wouldn't happen. Still, when Sally Holland set out to find a prom dress, she didn't think her life would take an unexpected and, possibly, tragic turn. Who would?

If something wicked had taken up residence in Foxglove Corners, I resolved to find it and send it packing.

With a little help.

Twenty

Brent was waiting in the driveway when I arrived at home. He wasn't alone. I could barely make out the form of a large dog crouching in the back seat. She seemed determined to blend into the upholstery.

Rainbow?

He reached through the window of his vintage Plymouth to stroke the head of the trembling black collie. "I think I have Rainbow."

The dog's ears lay flat against her head, and her dark eyes were wary. At her right shoulder, a narrow swath of black fur splashed through her white collar.

I had never set eyes on Rainbow. Did Ellalyn's dog have a broken collar? It would be a certain way of identifying her. Darn. I couldn't ask Ellalyn and couldn't call Rainbow's picture to mine.

She had been groomed at the shelter and wore a new pink collar, but she seemed thin to me. Almost scrawny. How long had she been missing?

"Rainbow," Brent said. "What a good girl!"

The collie didn't respond. She stood but kept her ears and tail well hidden.

"I don't think so," I said. "We now have two tris and neither one is Rainbow."

"Well, even if this isn't the right dog, the people up in Maple Falls let me take her. They think she'll have a better chance of finding a new home in a more populated area."

"I'm glad you brought her," I said. "If by chance this is Rainbow, how did she get all the way up to Maple Falls, I wonder?"

"Whoever took her dumped her there."

"And we're back to the basic question. Why?"

Neither of us had an answer.

"What did they call her at the shelter?" I asked.

"Blackie."

"How unoriginal. Let's call her…Let's see. Raina. Whoever adopts her will give her another name. Poor confused baby."

"Raina," Brent repeated. "It doesn't sound right. Too exotic. How about Rainy?"

"Let Sue decide." Noticing the collie was panting, I said, "Let me get her a drink."

"Yeah. She polished off all the bottles I brought."

When I came back with the water in one of the dogs' bowls, Brent said, "I'll drop her off at Sue's and come back for dinner. What are we having?"

I had no idea. Crane could grill chicken, I supposed. I'd make a salad and bake biscuits, and together we'd make a new plan.

"It's a surprise," I said, thinking of the blueberry pie I'd baked this morning.

Life was proving to be full of surprises.

While we were trying so hard to find Ellalyn's dog, Ellalyn had slipped off the canvas. The mystery kept growing.

~ * ~

During dinner, Brent said, "You'd think we were living in the Wild West. I stopped off for a burger and took a wrong turn. Getting back to the right road, I passed an old farmhouse with about twenty trucks parked in front. It sounded like there was a battle going on behind the place. Lots of gunfire."

"Was this in Foxglove Corners?" Crane asked.

"About an hour from the border. Poor Rainy started crying."

"Maybe target practice?"

"What else? Target practice with a small army. Believe me, I didn't stay to find out."

"An hour north of here?" Crane asked.

"About that. Northwest of I-75."

"I think I'll check it out."

"You do that, Sheriff."

"Some people think they can do anything they like in the country," I said. "I'm so glad we have quiet neighbors."

I glanced at the platter of chicken. It needed refilling, and I needed a brief time-out from gun talk. Usually, the memory of the Marston shooting remained buried in my mind, but at times, it resurfaced. Like tonight.

Along with the shooting and the boy who had lost his life, I remembered the aftermath, the sound of gunfire I had heard at odd times and in various places when no one else did.

The haunting.

I hated guns. I knew Crane needed to carry a weapon, but I was happier when it was locked in its special cabinet next to the gun I'd bought for emergencies.

In my opinion, too many people owned guns. They were too handy when volatile persons found themselves in disagreement. Children could find them and harm or even kill one another, and far too many people insisted on carrying them as if they were fashion accessories.

In the kitchen, I transferred the rest of the chicken to the platter under the watchful eyes of eight collies.

"You'll get yours later," I promised. "There's plenty."

Candy gave a piteous whine and did her best to trip me as I went back to the living room. To the men I said, "More chicken?"

"I'm good," Crane said. "Save room for pie, Fowler."

"There's always room for Jennet's pie." Brent reached for a drumstick. "We need Ellalyn to identify Rainbow," he added. "Sue can't offer the collie I brought back from Maple Falls for adoption if she has an owner."

"I've left plenty of messages for Ellalyn but only went to her house once."

"Maybe a neighbor can tell you where she went," Crane said.

I thought of that quiet street. No one outside tending to their lawn. No one coming or going. No children playing; not even a dog in sight. "I'll go again as soon as I have an hour or so free," I said.

I could knock on a few doors and ask some discreet questions or go back to the Green House of Antiques and talk to another salesperson. Maybe Zara, the new co-owner.

School would be over soon, the last exam given, the last grades calculated and submitted, and we'd all disperse for the summer vacation. I frowned as I recalled the threat written on my blackboard. I could only hope I'd leave my ill-wisher behind in Oakpoint.

Meanwhile, I looked forward to relaxing on the porch with a good Gothic novel in my hands and a glass of lemonade on the table. Miss Eidt and I would also be visiting Joanne Linder.

Would I possibly learn something new from Joanne about the cold case disappearance of Celia Loring?

Unlikely after all these years, but I didn't like to leave even a single stone unturned.

Twenty-one

The last day of school arrived with a threat of rain lurking in the gray low-lying clouds. Teachers would have a workday tomorrow without students, and the building would resemble a vast echoing structure in a ghost town.

Don't think about ghosts, I told myself as I counted the exams destined for my fifth period American Lit class. The last exam, as I didn't have a sixth hour.

Think of peace and quiet. No interruptions. Storing books and materials for another year. Think of tomorrow.

But every now and then, I turned to check that the blackboard still retained its pristine state.

Did you expect a second warning to materialize?

Satisfied there was no imminent danger, I gazed at the view from the window, property owned by the school and left in its natural state. Draped in shades of early summer green, the ten acres were home to a rarely-seen herd of deer.

In ten minutes, my class would come into the room, most likely in serious mode. There would be fewer today as the seniors had graduated. I didn't know where Rusty was, didn't care, and hoped he wouldn't break through the hall monitors' defenses to accost me in my room during my conference period.

He wouldn't dare show up. On the other hand, the hall monitors were released from duty.

Tomorrow, I intended to work with Leonora in her classroom, which had once been my own, the scene of the shooting.

Stop! Leave it in the past.

I rose and closed the window nearest my desk. In spite of the muggy weather, the room had grown unaccountably cool.

Something's going to happen.

The voice was pure imagination, originating in the furthest recesses of my mind, home of unwanted memories. A series of images rolled by: pictures of the Marston shooter, of the boy on the floor, and the teacher in the next room who appeared at the door moments later, of terrified faces and blood.

The bell rang, and I turned away from the doomsday camera roll in my mind.

Let the last show begin.

~ * ~

Thunder rumbled over Oakpoint.

I stood at the window surveying the class. They were quieter than they'd ever been, for once everyone hard at work on the last test of the course. No one needed help or had an emergency like a pen that suddenly went dry.

I had purposely made the exam long lest they finish early and get restless. The rules were clear. No hall passes. No early dismissals. Read over your work. Take a nap. Just be quiet.

Forty-five minutes left, and so far, so good.

My foreboding could be a product of the weather, the building storm, the sudden lightning flash.

After all, what could go wrong?

Anything.

The building could take a direct lightning hit. A warning could mysteriously form itself on the blackboard. A bomb could go off. Or I'd get through the day safely only to find my car missing from the parking lot.

You are going to drive yourself insane.

One of the girls looked up from her test, staring fearfully out the window. I sent her a reassuring smile.

As it happened, the exam period passed without incident. The rain came and moved north, leaving a sparkling vista. The bell rang. My students left the room for the last time, and I stashed their tests in the closet and locked the door.

One more possibility occurred to me. The tests could disappear.

All right. Then it would be my secret. Everyone would receive an 'A.'

I took my lunch out of the top drawer and went next door to meet Leonora.

~ * ~

Many of the staff took the opportunity of a longer break to go out to eat, but Leonora and I opted to have one more lunch in the courtyard. By this time tomorrow, we would be on the way home.

Leonora produced a towel and ran it over the bench.

"It's sad," I said.

"What?"

"The courtyard. Flowerbeds raked for the last time; the fountain turned off. I loved relaxing to the sound of falling water."

"Speaking of which, Jake and I are going up to Mackinac Island, then on to the Upper Peninsula this weekend," Leonora said.

She waited for me to reveal my plans.

"We're staying home."

I thought of my porch, of reading through my latest Gothic gatherings, of playing with my collies, and playing detective. It was every bit as appealing as a long car trip.

Scenes inspired by my premonition had all but faded. Still, the slightest note of unease trembled in a corner of my mind. I told Leonora about my apprehension.

"Well, nothing happened, and it isn't likely to. Your last class has dispersed forever."

"I don't think the threat comes from one of my current students," I said.

"You're still worried that Rusty kid is out for revenge?"

"Maybe."

"Listen. He didn't graduate. It's a fact. He went on to other pursuits. Right now, he's probably heading for Sandy Point with a bunch of his buddies. You're ancient history to him."

I laughed. "Not ancient, surely."

"Don't obsess about it." She took a brownie out of her lunch. It was almost too pretty to eat, decorated with little gold stars glittering on dark chocolate frosting.

"This is for you," she said. "To celebrate one more successful ending."

We began eating. Sun glittered on the new-washed leaves and grass. Sunshine, sparkle, and glorious fresh air. The premonition lay still, melting in the heat of the day.

I should be at ease, all apprehension cast away. It—whatever it was—hadn't happened today.

But it was on the way.

Twenty-two

The next day, a half day for all except those teachers who hadn't completed their work, I gathered my exams, grade sheets, and gradebook, closed the windows, and prepared to lock my classroom door for the last time this school year.

Before leaving the room, I glanced at the blackboard. It was newly cleaned, chalk and erasers stored in the closet. No message flashed a warning at me in blood-red chalk.

Let it appear, I thought. *I won't be around to see it.*

The year was really over. I could consign disturbing memories to the past. Strangely, I hadn't thought Rusty would go so completely away. But I was glad he had.

I stood in the hall outside the door and let my mind fade to blank. If another premonition was going to appear, now was the time. It didn't. I was home free.

The hall was empty, classroom doors closed, absolutely silent. Leonora was already in the library, waiting with the others for the end-of-the-school-year meeting to begin.

I slid into a chair beside her. This gathering was mere formality. A tradition. There was a general air of restlessness and relief, and a strong odor of lemon furniture polish.

"Where's the cake?" I murmured.

"There isn't any," Leonora said.

"Why?"

That was the other part of the tradition. On the last day, the cafeteria ladies served cake with tea, coffee, or soft drinks. There was no sign of any refreshment or anyone from the cafeteria, for that matter.

Mallory from the History Department overheard us.

"Diane has been sick. They're short-handed in the kitchen."

"Didn't anyone ever hear of a bakery?" I asked.

"We can get our own cake," Leonora said. "Shhh. He's going to speak."

Grimsley stood behind the librarian's desk. He wore his too-cheerful pasted-on smile and a gray striped tie that seemed to be too tight. While he tugged at it and waited for the staff to quiet down, I glanced at the clock behind him. We would have two free hours today, one for lunch at Clovers and one to visit the Green House of Antiques.

"So we come to the end of another year," the principal was saying. "Thank you all for your hard work. Have a good rest and come back in September energized and ready to make next year even better."

And that was it? This was by far the shortest meeting we'd ever attended. That was okay. The day was warm perfection, and golden sunbeams slipped through the windows, calling us to come out and play.

People were rising, exchanging wishes for a happy summer. Coach Adam Barrett was already out the door. It was really, really over. I wished I had a handful of confetti to throw in the air.

Leonora and I joined the mass exodus to the parking lot. "Tomorrow, I'm going shopping for new vacation clothes," Leonora said. "What are you going to do?"

"Tomorrow I'll..." I paused. "I'll tackle my summer mysteries."

"Rainbow, you mean?"

"And Celia Loring. Also, I hope to finish my ghost book."

Some time ago, I had started writing stories about the supernatural manifestations I'd experienced since moving to Foxglove Corners.

Neither one of my current mysteries contained a ghost. As far as I knew.

Unless you considered Woodside Park a character in itself, rather like the moor in *Wuthering Heights*.

I liked that idea. A park of many mysteries assuming the role of a villainous spirit.

But it wouldn't be part of my book unless I found Rainbow and learned what had happened to Celia. And unless there was a supernatural connection to one or both.

~ * ~

Annica wasn't working at Clovers. After a lunch of sandwiches, lime coolers, and lemon chiffon cake, we moved on to the Green House of Antiques.

The street known as Antique Row drowsed in the mid-day sun. It was a pleasure to slow down and window shop at our leisure. We had time to stop at the other antique shops on the Row, but I couldn't wait to browse among the series books at the Green House and learn more about Ellalyn, if possible.

The window presented the same 'fun at the beach' tableau to admiring passersby that I'd seen on my last visit. The keeper of the window had changed the dolls' wardrobes and added books to the collection.

Leonora said, "That bathing suit over there was considered rather risqué in the olden days."

"I wonder where they found the outfit. It looks new."

"Some grandmother's attic? I need a new swimsuit for our trip. A more modern style, naturally."

"And I need answers."

I opened the door to the tinkling of the seashell chimes and stood for a moment, adjusting to the dim interior and cool air.

I said, "Wouldn't it be nice if Ellalyn were here?"

I didn't see her, and didn't expect to, but today's salesperson was none other than the co-owner, Zara, and we were her only customers. What a stroke of luck!

She wore a full navy skirt that skimmed her ankles and a lacy white blouse with three gold chains. I didn't know what decade she represented, but she looked sufficiently old-fashioned to complement her wares.

She wouldn't know I'd previously expressed an interest in Ellalyn's whereabouts. Therefore, I could ask about her again with impunity.

"Good afternoon, ladies," she said. "What can I show you?"

"Do you have any Tiffany lamps?" Leonora asked.

"Several gorgeous ones at reasonable prices. You'll find them displayed throughout the shop."

"I was hoping to talk to Ellalyn," I said. "Is she working today?"

Zara hesitated and pulled lightly on her chains. A nervous gesture, I assumed, as she proceeded to twist them around her fingers.

"Ellalyn is on a short leave. She should return at the end of the month. Would you like to leave a message?"

I had already left several on her phone. She hadn't answered one.

"I heard she was on vacation, but I also heard she'd resigned. I thought she'd be back by now."

I'd heard no such thing.

"Her boyfriend needed her to go somewhere with him," Zara said.

Boyfriend? Here was my chance to add to my knowledge, if Zara would cooperate.

"You must be talking about—John. John Smith."

"No, Garth."

"Garth?"

"Garth MacKay."

"I guess I'll have to see her when she comes back," I said.

"About your message?" Zara asked.

"Mmm. I'll wait.

Zara turned to Leonora. "Let me show you a lamp I especially like. Do you like yellow lilies?"

"That's my favorite color and my favorite flower," Leonora said.

As Zara led Leonora to the back of the store, I checked nearby tables for series books, but my mind was on Ellalyn, and the various tales swirling around her whereabouts.

Her precious collie had been stolen, but instead of joining in the search, she had left town with a boyfriend she had never mentioned.

But why would she mention him to me? We weren't friends; we were barely acquaintances.

What was the real story? And, most important of all, where was Ellalyn now?

Twenty-three

"Rainbow vanishes, stolen from her crate, and Ellalyn drops out of sight, presumably to take a trip with her boyfriend," I said. "I don't understand. It's like she doesn't care about her dog."

"You're obviously not hearing the full story," Miss Eidt said.

"I'm hearing what Zara wanted me to know."

But Zara hadn't said anything about Rainbow.

"It *is* odd that Ellelyn would take a leave of absence from her job at this time," Miss Eidt said. "So soon after taking a vacation, I mean. If that's what she did."

"Zara said Ellalyn would return to work at the end of June."

"Unless Rainbow drops back in sight, you can't do anything until you talk to Ellalyn," Miss Eidt pointed out.

She was right. In the meantime, I could enjoy the scenery and my first outing of the summer with Miss Eidt, who rarely left the library or her neat little house close by.

She wasn't closing the library, having faith in her assistant's ability to keep it running smoothly in her absence.

We had entered Maple Creek and were driving along Main Street, which was famous for its elegant Victorians and the maple trees that shaded them. Everything in sight was green and bursting with vibrant new life.

"Do you think Joanne will mind talking about her niece?" I asked.

"Oh, my goodness, not at all. At one time, that was all she wanted to talk about. She seemed to believe that by reliving that day, she'd remember something important. It never happened."

"There's always a first time, and a person unfamiliar with the story might notice something off. Maybe..."

I broke off as I drove past a majestic lavender Victorian house turned business establishment. A sign on a rocky mound in front identified it as Sky and MacKay Title.

MacKay. That wasn't the most common of surnames. Could it be...?

"Zara told me that Ellalyn's boyfriend's name is Garth MacKay."

"Several people in Foxglove Corners share a surname," Miss Eidt said. "Like Zoller. I know six Zollers besides Ellalyn, none of whom are related."

"It's probably a coincidence," I said.

Possibly, but could it be a clue to Rainbow's disappearance? I wondered if I could fabricate a need for a title expert before leaving Maple Creek.

"Joanne lives on this street," Miss Eidt reminded me. "A little further down. Ah, there it is."

Joanne's house was pale lavender with purple gingerbread trim, although it was somewhat smaller than the title Victorian. A profusion of pink gardenias blossomed on the porch beneath six hanging baskets filled with trailing ivy.

"And there's Joanne," Miss Eidt said.

She was watering her plants. A petite lady in a bright floral-patterned sundress with silver waves tumbling out from a straw sunhat, she reminded me of Camille.

I parked, and we met her halfway down the winding walkway to the porch. Joanne enveloped Miss Eidt in a long hug.

"Elizabeth!" she cried. "It's been too long. You're looking so well and...you have a new ring. It's magnificent."

She was looking at Miss Eidt's engagement ring, whose diamonds appeared to catch every sunbeam in its depth.

"Yes," she said. "I love it. After all these years, I've found the perfect man. We're getting married next spring."

"I am so very happy for you," Joanne said. "I want to know all about him."

"You will, but first, I want you to meet Jennet."

Joanne grasped my hand. "The young lady who's interested in my Celia."

"Not out of morbid curiosity," I said quickly and explained about Rainbow's disappearance.

She shuddered. "That awful park. Sometimes I still dream about it."

"I've never been there," Miss Eidt admitted.

"You don't want to go."

"Let's get in out of the sun," Joanne said. "I have pitchers of iced tea and a new drink with pineapple, lemonade, and Sprite, if you'd like to try it."

When we were inside, seated at an elegant mahogany dining room table set for a high tea, I said, "Joanne, I wonder if you know one of your neighbors, the man in the title house down the street?"

"Only to say hello to. Garth MacKay is rather intimidating with that black beard. Why do you ask?"

His name was Garth. I felt I was getting closer to—something.

"Supposedly he's a special friend of Rainbow's owner, who's gone missing herself," I said.

"I don't know anything about the gentleman's personal life," Joanne said. "I used to see him walking with a pretty young woman who had long black hair."

That wasn't Ellalyn, unless she'd changed her appearance and colored her hair.

"It's probably irrelevant," I said.

I didn't really think so, but we had come together to talk about the disappearance of Celia Loring. I moved Garth MacKay a space down my list. I'd deal with him later.

"Celia was my only niece," Joanne said. "I was her godmother. We were very close, right from the day she was born. To lose her like that broke my heart. And not to know what became of her. The pain goes on and on. She would be a grown woman now," she added. "Celia would be beautiful, kind, accomplished..."

She trailed off, staring into space, no doubt seeing Celia grown.

Abruptly, she left the table and came back with a framed picture of an enchanting golden-haired child wearing a blue jumper and carrying a stuffed toy spaniel.

"Nutmeg, one of her favorites," Joanne said.

"Would you tell me about the day she disappeared?" I asked.

"Gladly," she said. "When I talk about Celia, I can almost bring her back to life. At least for a little while."

I took a sip of Joanne's lemonade-pineapple drink and sat back in the chair while she slipped with ease into the past.

Joanne's Story

The day Celia disappeared was the worst day of my life, and I've never stopped blaming myself. If only we'd gone to the movies instead of the park, or gone shopping. Celia loved to shop.

She often spent the night with me, and sometimes she came over during the day. We played and read books together and took picnic lunches to Woodsboro Park. Celia loved the swings and the fountain. The fountain is gone now, but that's another story.

I remember how hot it was the day she vanished. It looked like all the kids in the neighborhood were at the park trying to cool off. Celia was wearing the pink sundress I'd made for her. It was deep pink and easy to spot.

After we ate our sandwiches, she joined some of her friends at the slides. Five little girls and a grubby boy in a torn shirt. I watched her slide down three or four times. She stood on the ground for a few seconds, waved to me, then ran over to the swings. That's the last time I saw her, my last memory. Running toward the swings.

The heat was giving me a headache, and it was hard to breathe. I felt like I were inhaling fire.

I closed my eyes, just for a minute. The last thing I remembered was music coming from the ice cream truck. I remember the tune, 'The Arkansas Traveler.' I could still hear it, but it was far away.

And it was so noisy in the park. Kids were screaming the way they do when they're running around and having fun. I looked for Celia in the crowd, looked for her pink dress but didn't see her.

I wasn't worried or afraid. Not then. Not yet.

I remembered wondering if she'd gone into the woods. I hoped not. The boys loved to play there. They'd pretend they were on an adventure or big game hunters. But Celia usually stayed near the play equipment.

I saw her friend, Maryanne, and walked over to ask her if she knew where Celia was.

"Don't know," she said. "She was just here. I asked her if she wanted to get a cone."

"Did she?"

"She said she'd ask her aunt."

Of course she would. I had the money.

"But she didn't come to me," I said. "I didn't see her."

"Yeah. Well, then, I don't know."

That was when I began to be afraid.

I questioned every child in sight. Everyone knew Celia; nobody could tell me where she was.

Time seemed to speed up. There were fewer children in the park then and I didn't see any other adults. No one was walking a dog. It was suddenly deathly quiet. The kids had stopped screaming. Why on earth was that? Because the ice cream truck was gone, and they were busy eating cones?

A woman I didn't know touched my arm. "You're looking for your little girl? Cecile?"

"Celia," I said. "A little blonde girl in a pink dress. Did you see her?"

"No, but I'll help you look. I'm Marigold Asher."

We looked everywhere, in places I'd already searched. Needless to say, we didn't find her.

I felt ill. My headache was raging with pain behind each eye. I was going to be sick. I had to go home, but I had to find Celia first. I couldn't leave without her.

Where was she?

A wicked voice whispered in my mind: *Not here. Gone. She's never coming back.*

I was more afraid at that moment than I'd ever been before.

Twenty-four

My throat had gone dry, with the icy drink cooling and unnoticed at my elbow. It was as if I had been the one talking. I took a long sip as Joanne continued her story.

"Ever since that day, I've waited to hear that Celia has been found," Joanne said. "Somebody has to have faith. Her mother and most people, the ones who still remember her, believe she's dead, that whoever took her killed her that day or soon after. As for myself, I'll never stop believing."

Miss Eidt wiped her eyes with a tissue. "But why would this kidnapper choose one little girl among all the other children in the park that day?"

"I've thought about that and decided it had to be random. Maybe the man or woman was closer to Celia than any of the other children."

I didn't think it had happened that way. I said, "But why didn't Celia cry out? Why didn't anyone notice her being removed from the park?

"Like that girl, Maryanne," Miss Eidt said. "From what you said, they were planning to get ice cream cones."

The incident was an eerie echo of how Rainbow had gone missing in a crowded park. Had I really hoped to find a clue to Celia's disappearance when over the years no one had?

"What did you do then? I asked.

"I stayed in the park until almost dark with Marigold, who turned out to be a neighbor. People came and went. One kind man helped me search the woods. If this had happened today, I would have called the police on my cell phone immediately. One of the mothers notified them. But it was clear. Celia wasn't there. It was as if a hand had come out from another dimension and grabbed her."

That could have happened in a science-fiction story, but this was life. All signs indicated a predator had snatched Celia and spirited her away.

"By that time my sister, Jane, had joined us," Joanne said. "She'd been wondering why I hadn't brought Celia home and took a chance we'd be in the park. She kept telling me she didn't blame me, but I knew she did, deep down. To this day, twenty years later, there's an unspoken barrier between us."

"How sad," Miss Eidt said. "Families should pull together in times of tragedy."

"Yes, but it happened on my watch. I don't blame her. I can't forgive myself."

"Keep the faith," Miss Eidt added. "It's never too late. Someday I pray you'll know what happened to Celia and, someday, you may be reunited with her."

Hollow words, but they seemed to cheer Joanne.

"Someday," she echoed.

~ * ~

I drove slowly down Main Street to the title company and pulled in the driveway. The grounds were neatly landscaped and well shaded with mature maple trees, but the grass needed mowing. It didn't look as if any one was home.

Still, I rapped softly on the door. Miss Eidt stood quietly beside me, observing a planter filled with candy cane striped geraniums, the only flowers in sight.

"What are you hoping for?" she asked in a whisper.

"A few minutes with Garth MacKay. I'll say he was recommended to me by—"

The door opened, and a pretty young woman regarded us warily. She was casually attired in a full white skirt and a mint green sweater whose soft color matched her eyes.

Behind her, I glimpsed an interior that resembled a tastefully furnished living room rather than the office I'd envisioned. A portrait held pride of place above the mantel. A man with a black beard, a girl who resembled the one in front of us, and a ferocious looking dog, all three posed in front of the purple Victorian.

The man was strikingly handsome and, as Joanne had said, intimidating with his black beard, in vivid contrast to the smiling young woman at his side.

"Good afternoon," I said. "I'd like to speak to Mr. Garth MacKay."

She kept her hand on the doorknob. "I'm sorry. Mr. MacKay is out of the office, but I expect Mr. Sky shortly. You didn't have an appointment?"

"No, I only learned about the company recently. I'll be in need of their services soon, and I was told to deal with Garth MacKay."

"I can make you an appointment," the young woman said. "Mr. MacKay will be in next week."

Did I want that? Certainly. Maple Creek wasn't that far away. The fact that Mr. MacKay and Ellalyn were away at the same time was significant.

The living room contained a large oak desk with neat stacks of papers and a shiny brass nameplate indicating that the owner was Taryn MacKay.

His wife, perhaps? Did Ellalyn know Garth was married? If he was.

Taryn flipped through an engagement book. "Mr. MacKay can see you on Monday morning. Would ten-thirty be all right?"

"Perfect," I said. "Thank you."

That would give me ample time to concoct a credible story.

I glanced at Miss Eidt. "We'll be on our way, then."

The young woman ushered us to the door, lingering for a moment on the threshold as if to soak in the heavenly breeze. "Lovely day, isn't it?"

"Perfect," I said. "I'll see you next week."

Back in the car, Miss Eidt sighed heavily. "That was a disappointment."

"Not really. It's a case of gratification delayed. I'll be well prepared when I show up for the appointment."

"You'll also be extra careful, I hope."

"No need in this case. I'll be a potential client. Why do you think there's danger?"

"There's no specific reason, but I have a feeling."

So did I, but I hadn't acknowledged it yet.

"We've been spending too much time with Lucy Hazen," I said. "Speaking of Lucy, I've been thinking about asking her to go to the park with me."

"Why would you do that? You said *I* shouldn't go."

I smiled, noting we were leaving the outskirts of Maple Creek. I was suddenly eager to be back home.

"You should stay safe in the library. You have a wedding coming up."

"Next year."

"Don't worry about me," I said. "I won't go alone."

As if that could keep me safe.

Twenty-five

In my dream, I wandered through the wooded section of the park with Misty, dodging low-hanging branches that reached out to grab me. Gnarled tree roots rose high from the ground, and rapacious vines wound themselves around my ankles.

I was treading a true obstacle course. Any moment I would fall. I looked for a trunk to hold on to, but the trees slipped away from me, enveloped in a growing white mist. The mosquitoes were thick and thirsty, and an ominous buzz circled around me.

I was lost in the woods and under attack.

Lost in a park? How likely was that?

The happy cries of children at play found their way through the tangle of wildlife, mixing with a tinny tune I recognized from third grade singing class:

Far and far away down in Arkansas
There lived a squatter with a stubborn jaw
His nose was ruby red and his whiskers gray
And he would sit and fiddle all the night and all the day.

Nonsensical words with a catchy melody that yanked me out of the woods and deposited me in the play area, precariously balanced on a swing. I grasped the ropes on either side, moving up, up and up, higher and higher, toward the sky. I was going to land on the puffy white cloud that lay so close to the treetops it was almost within reach.

But where had Misty gone? I didn't see her.

Instead of the cloud, the swing flung me into a graveyard at the foot of an odd statue atop a grave, a stone girl sitting on a stone bench. What an unusual and bizarre choice of a memorial.

I woke to moonlight pouring through the bedroom window, to heavy breathing at the side of the bed. Misty. I was home and safe.

I had been thinking too much about Woodsboro Park, and that was most likely a waste of time. Celia had vanished from the park years ago, as had Rainbow. There was no chance the two disappearances were connected, separated as they were by decades. No chance at all.

So what was the point of revisiting the park?

A premonition of the 'no stones unturned' kind?

Darn. Now I was thirsty.

Quietly, I left our bed, took the small flashlight from my nightstand drawer, and stepped over Halley, who lay in the doorway. Misty was already halfway down the stairs.

My house, so familiar to me, so well-loved, seemed strange in the dark of night, another place entirely. All shadows and silence and unexplored corners.

I turned on the kitchen light and checked the time on the microwave. Twenty minutes past midnight. I should have stayed in bed, because now a cup of cocoa and a muffin held more appeal than fruit juice. By the time I had both, I'd be wide awake.

I reached for a saucepan and the cocoa tin. Candy appeared at my side, nudging Misty out of the way, no doubt hoping for a second bedtime snack.

Unfortunately, I couldn't stop the thoughts that careened through my mind, clamoring for attention. As I measured cocoa into the boiling water, I gave them free rein.

There was no chance of learning Celia's fate after all these years, but Rainbow was another story. That mystery was relatively new, and, after our trip to Maple Creek, I knew slightly more about it now.

Ellalyn had vanished. Garth MacKay was away from his business, presumably out of town. According to Zara at the Green House of Antiques, Garth and Ellalyn were together, which meant Garth was a legitimate lead, one to be pursued in the morning.

I'd launch a search for him on the Internet. I wanted to know something of his background before our appointment.

~ * ~

Crane came in surrounded by a pack of prancing collies eager to see what would come next. He said, "The kitchen looks different, honey. Brighter."

"It's summer, and the sun is out."

I'd covered the oak table with a yellow gingham checked tablecloth and matching napkins. Crane looked bright himself with the early morning sunlight dancing off his badge and turning the strands in his blond hair to silver.

I beat eggs into a froth and dipped a slice of bread in the mixture. French toast would complement the decor.

Crane stepped around Candy and pulled out an oak chair. "Do you have any plans for today?"

"I'm going to stay home and see if I can gather some facts about Ellalyn's boyfriend, Garth MacKay."

Crane frowned. "That name sounds familiar."

"He has a title business in Maple Creek."

I turned the bread over and watched it turn golden-brown, stepped back, and almost trod on Candy's paw.

"That isn't it. Let me think. It'll come to me."

When the French toast was ready, I refilled his coffee cup and joined him at the table.

"Why are you interested in Garth MacKay?" he asked.

"He's a link to Ellalyn and through him to Rainbow."

"That sounds like a pretty weak link."

"I don't have anything else."

"Be careful,' he said.

"There's no danger in looking for a lost dog."

"A stolen dog," he reminded me. "Until we find out why Ellalyn's collie was taken and where she is now, I want you to keep a low profile."

"If it were any lower, I'd be off the canvas," I said and passed him the syrup.

My plan for the day involved sitting on the porch with the dogs and my laptop. What could be safer than that?

~ * ~

The collies joined me on the porch, most of them settling into early morning naps. Except for Misty and Candy. They lay close together at the foot of the stairs, their eyes fixed on the woods across the lane, ready for a deer or coyote sighting. Or something.

I let my eyes rest on the green panorama of leaves swaying in a light wind and turned back to the screen, where I'd clicked on the website of Sky and MacKay Title.

It had a clean, sparse design in cool blue and white with a picture of the purple Victorian draped in snow. The site included a scattering of reviews, all favorable.

However, I also discovered multiple entries for both Garth MacKay and his partner, Greg Sky, along with a brief article which hinted at vague ties to the Michigan Militia.

I looked away from the screen, hoping to find inspiration in the wind-tossed woodscape across Jonquil Lane. I was under the impression the Michigan Militia had been disbanded, mostly because I hadn't read or heard about their activities in ages.

How naive. They could have moved underground. I had no doubt that Crane would eventually remember where he had heard of Garth MacKay and suspected that it was in connection with this subversive group.

Perhaps there *was* an element of danger in my quest.

Twenty-six

An hour later, Annica and I sat at my favorite booth in Clovers over sandwiches and lime coolers, discussing Garth MacKay, a man neither of us had ever met.

"Do you suppose Ellalyn knows her boyfriend has ties to the Michigan Militia?" Annica asked. "If he does, that is."

I swirled my straw through the last half of my drink. "It depends. Would a man share that part of his life with a girlfriend? It would depend on how recent the relationship is, how close they were, and other things."

All information we had no way of knowing.

Annica drained her glass and glanced at the soda fountain. These delicious lime coolers didn't last half as long as they should.

"I can't see it," she added. "A quiet lady who works with antiques and a militia man. I thought that group was an antique, something that had fallen apart in the distant past."

"Nothing like that ever goes completely away," I said. "Ellalyn seemed a trifle old-fashioned to me." I added the segue because the unlikely pairing puzzled me.

I wasn't remembering Ellalyn at the park, but in the Green House, clad in vintage attire, surrounded by relics of a bygone time. How to reconcile that image with the rough, tough figure of a man who lived his life according to his own code.

"Some women are attracted to dangerous men," Annica said.

"From his picture, I can say he's very attractive, if you like a man with a beard. I don't."

"Me neither. Brent is my idea of the perfect man. Oh, and Crane, too. He's kind of perfect."

Her allusion to Brent reminded me of a story I'd disregarded as insignificant at the time. But was it?

"When Brent went up north to see if the tri in Maple Falls was Rainbow, he took a wrong turn on the way back, and came across an old farmhouse where people were shooting. Dozens of them, from the sound of the gunfire. He didn't stop to investigate, but I wonder. Was something nefarious going on there?"

We fell quiet. After a while, Annica said, "It might have been a target shooting party. Do you think Brent could find that place again?"

"Probably," I said. "Or Crane could."

"Or *we* could."

"No!"

Crane was always warning me about hazardous undertakings. He wouldn't have to warn me about this one. Keeping my appointment with Garth MacKay, pretending to need a title expert, was fairly innocuous. And I intended to go no further.

Annica said, "I always thought we lived in a peaceful part of the state."

So did I, but...Woods and lakes, old Victorian houses, and two strange roads that defied the laws of nature. Ghost stories and ghostly apparitions.

"Sometimes peace is an illusion," I said.

~ * ~

When I returned home, I leashed Halley, Sky, and Star, my easy-to-walk girls, and set out for Sue Appleton's horse ranch.

The wind had died down, but rustling leaves on either side of Jonquil Lane created a sense of unease. Did something stir in the woods? Or someone?

It's only a creature, I told myself. *Maybe a fox or—horrors--a coyote. Nothing human.*

I smiled at the notion of a militiaman lurking in the ruins of the abandoned construction site. Surely that wasn't sufficiently underground. An occasional vagrant in search of shelter from the elements took advantage of the falling-apart structures. The acres were private but not secret.

A swishing sound caught the collies' attention. And mine. Then a snapping sound I couldn't identify.

Nothing. A bird?

We walked on, turning right at Squill Lane, and continued on to Sue's place. She was outside playing with her collies—all of them. I looked for Pepper in the swirl of fur and saw her leaping to catch a blue Frisbee. And there was Rainy, the tri Brent had brought back from the Maple Falls shelter. My three trembled and whined in their eagerness to join the game.

Pepper let Scarlet catch the Frisbee and came running up to greet me. She remembered me!

"She remembers," Sue said and gave my collies a round of pats. "Come sit on the porch."

We sank into cushioned wicker chairs on either side of a table laden with a pitcher of water and a dish of shortbread cookies. Of Sue's pack, only Pepper followed us, stretching out on the cool wood as if she'd lived with Sue since her puppyhood.

"I'm going to keep her, and somebody's interested in Rainy," Sue said. "Pepper is incredibly smart. I think she can read my mind. Someone trained her well."

"Only to give her away in a bizarre scheme."

"Yes. No one has inquired about her. I can't understand it.

"And Rainbow is still missing.

"She may never be found."

"I don't know what more we can do to look for her," I said. "Now her owner is gone, too, heaven knows where."

While Pepper drifted off into a light doze and my trio hovered around the dogs' jumbo-sized pail of water, I told Sue about Garth

MacKay and my discovery about his affiliation with the Michigan Militia.

"Zara at the Green House of Antiques said Ellalyn had gone away with her boyfriend, Garth MacKay."

"I thought MacKay's girlfriend was named Katherine, Katherine Kale," Sue said. "They must have broken up."

I almost dropped my cookie. "Do you know her?"

"I've met Katherine. She adopted one of my rescues, a pretty little tri girl."

Sometimes after a long, dry spell, opportunities drop into your lap. If Sue knew Garth's former girlfriend, perhaps she could introduce me to her. Maybe Katherine could be convinced to talk about Garth.

I could just picture that conversation. "What can you tell me about your ex, Katherine? Because I think he's involved in something shady."

That would be awkward. Ludicrous, actually, and unlikely to produce the desired result.

Still, it was a heaven-sent lead, and I resolved to pursue it.

Twenty-seven

The next day, home from shopping, I emptied the mailbox and drove on to the house. The collies had spotted me through the bay window and risen a clamor. I parked, let myself in, and dropped the mail on the kitchen table. Catalogs and bills—and a postcard that fell out with a glossy colored ad for the Farmers Market.

The postcard extolled one of the seven sights of Oakpoint, Michigan, a majestic oak tree said to be over a century old. Oddly, it had fallen in a high wind two years ago, and its replacement was a mere stripling. An old postcard, then.

I turned it over. Its message consisted of pasted-on letters cut from a newspaper: Three simple words and a question mark. *Who's sorry now?*

Misty sniffed at it and growled softly, while my mind traveled back to my classroom at Marston High School, to another three words written on the blackboard: *You'll be sorry!* Rusty's parting threat.

"Not again." I tossed the postcard aside. I had thought I'd left it all behind—the controversy about unearned credit for an aspiring graduate. Principal Grimley's obvious bias in favor of the student. The annoying pleas of Rusty's friends. I should have known he would continue his...his what? His vendetta?

Even though graduation was firmly entrenched in the past. Even though we'd gone our separate ways.

The postcard didn't have a stamp, which meant that someone, Rusty probably, had dropped it in my mailbox, which was illegal; but wasn't sending people threatening messages also illegal? If not, it should be.

I set it aside to show to Crane and started gathering ingredients to make a pasta salad. Crane was going to grill steaks, and we had half of yesterday's pie left for dessert.

As I worked, I thought about the question on the postcard. *Who's sorry now?* Certainly not I.

I hadn't changed my mind about giving Rusty a passing grade for a course virtually unattended. If I had yielded to pressure and given him even a 'D-', that would have been a lie and allowed him to go out into the world believing the school had only given him his due. Life didn't work that way. I was a teacher, and sometimes lessons were unpalatable.

As for his threats, they were vague. Unspecified. Possibly only hateful words. He couldn't hurt me. Could he? I would wait to see what Crane had to say.

~ * ~

Crane examined the postcard and set it on the counter. "It isn't exactly a threat, but whoever delivered it was on our property, and it's addressed to you. You think the culprit is this kid from your class?"

"Former class," I pointed out. "The seniors graduated. Rusty didn't. He blames me."

"Instead of himself."

"I thought once school was over, he'd forget about it. Well..." I paused, remembering Rusty's entitled attitude as he demanded make-up work. "Maybe he's not the type to let a grudge go."

"If that's so, you made another enemy," he said.

"A kid."

"Don't underestimate a kid with a grievance."

"I won't. What do you think I should do?"

"Be aware. Find out where he is now and what he's doing. Can you do that?"

"I can try. Someone must know. And meanwhile, he springs his trap."

"Let's hope he just wants to drive his point home. He wants you to feel guilty about not giving him his credit."

"I don't. Not a bit."

I wanted to be proactive and not wait for Rusty to creep up on me from the shadows. I wanted Crane to promise me that all would be well. He couldn't, of course. The future was uncertain. But Crane would be with me as would my eight collies, my pack of protection.

"Wish me luck," I said and handed him the steaks to take out to the grill.

I refused to live my life anticipating a terrible event that might never happen.

~ * ~

Once again, I entered Maple Creek and drove down its picturesque Main Street admiring the old Victorians that faced one another across the paved lanes and the mature maple trees that gave the town its name. We had arranged to have lunch with Katherine.

"You and Katherine have a lot in common," Sue said. "Katherine is a teacher in Capac, and her house has an interesting history. When she moved in, she discovered it was haunted."

"Was, not is? What happened?"

"You'll have to let Katherine tell you. It involved an unsolved murder. She doesn't usually talk about it, but she may if you mention your experiences."

"We don't want to lose sight of our goal," I said. "I'll see what she can tell us about Garth MacKay first."

As we passed Sky and MacKay Title, Sue said, "What a gorgeous house! I love the color. It doesn't look very busy, does it?"

That was an understatement. Not a single car was parked in the driveway. The place looked as if it were closed. Abandoned?

"Remember Garth MacKay is away somewhere," I said.

"Doesn't he have a partner, though?"

"I assume so."

And he had a secretary, Taryn MacKay. Wife or sister. But, as I said, there was no sign of a car. It was almost noon.

"Slow down," Sue said. "Katherine lives off Main Street on Walnut. She has a beautiful Victorian, too. Maple Creek is known for its vintage houses. I'd love to live in one, but I need land for my horses and dogs."

"Maple Creek is pretty, but in my opinion, we live in the best part of the state."

"This is it," Sue said, and I turned right on Walnut.

Katherine Kale's house was indeed an impressive Victorian, painted a soft shade of blue and trimmed with a wealth of gingerbread ornamentation. An added touch of beauty was the tricolor collie who greeted us from her fenced yard with a display of leaping, tail wagging, and barking.

"It's Diamond," Sue murmured. "She came to rescue from an owner who didn't want her and landed in collie heaven with Katherine. Katherine had just lost her dog, Vicky," she added, "so they were perfect for each other."

The young woman who opened the door was a great beauty with the long black hair described by Joanne Linder. Dressed in a simple white sheath with a flattering square neckline, she reminded me of a young Elizabeth Taylor without the dramatic makeup or extravagant jewelry. She didn't even wear a ring.

After enthusiastically greeting Sue, she turned to me.

"You're Jennet. I'm pleased to meet you..." Although she didn't add 'but,' it hung in the air. She seemed puzzled, as well she might be. I knew Sue hadn't told her about my interest in Garth MacKay.

She beckoned us inside, saying, "I'll let Diamond in. She loves company."

"I'd love to see her again," Sue said, and I was happy, for the dog's presence would be an admirable buffer.

Katherine opened the side door and the collie all but flew in and leaped at Sue. This was the first time I'd been ignored by a collie, and it felt strange. But Diamond's attention was for Sue alone.

Katherine reached for her collar. "Oh, I'm sorry. When she gets excited, she forgets her training."

"Don't worry," I said. "I'm used to exuberant collies."

Katherine glanced at the clock on the mantel. "It's still early for the Inn. Let's sit and talk for a while. Would you ladies like something to drink?"

"Water maybe," Sue said.

"That'd be nice." Not seeing the point in procrastinating, I said, "We're here because of Garth MacKay."

The room grew quiet. Even Diamond curbed her exuberance. Katherine ran her hand along Diamond's ribcage, not meeting my eyes.

"Because of a situation he may be involved in," I added. "A serious one that concerns us."

Still, she didn't speak.

I could see my hopes for enlightenment quickly fading away.

Twenty-eight

"I met him at the Apple Fair," Katherine said. "I had just moved to Maple Creek and we became friends. I narrowly escaped dying that day, but that's another story." She paused, gazing into space as if she were seeing that meeting unfolding before her eyes. "Perhaps Garth and I were more than friends, but in the end, it didn't work out."

"That's too bad," Sue said.

"What's your interest in Garth?" Katherine asked, her tone sharpening perceptibly.

This was my cue to talk, beginning with the disappearance of a collie from her crate during the Collie Walkabout.

"Now Rainbow's owner, Ellalyn, has gone missing, too," I said. "I understand Ellalyn was Garth MacKay's girlfriend, and he is away from his business."

"Ellalyn," Katherine murmured. "I wasn't aware...well, it's not my concern. You're implying that Garth and this Ellalyn are together, but what if they are?"

I let her question slide, hoping she wouldn't notice my evasion. "Is there any possibility Garth MacKay belongs to the Michigan Militia?" I asked.

Katherine frowned. Again, she paused. Sue fidgeted on her seat, her hand moving up and down Diamond's ruff.

"There's no such organization as the Michigan Militia," she said.

"I disagree. I've googled it."

"I don't know anything about Garth's activities," Katherine said. "We live in the same town, but I've scarcely seen him since we broke up."

I had a suspicion that Katherine knew very well that her erstwhile friend was a member of a dangerous group that did indeed exist. Could that be the reason for their separation?

"It's a mystery," I said. "The dog, her owner, her boyfriend—all missing. If these disappearances are related—"

"I'm sorry," she cut in. "I can't help you. But if Garth went somewhere with his new girlfriend, what does that have to do with his private affiliations? I don't understand the connection or your interest, now that I think of it."

I started as thunder rumbled over the house, adding a dramatic flourish to an awkward moment. Until then, it had been a picture-perfect summer day, and I'd neglected to listen to the weather report. The outside disturbance took our conversation in a different direction.

Perhaps we were both relieved.

Katherine rose. Diamond whimpered and slipped away from Sue, tearing out of the room.

"Diamond has a special place upstairs where she feels safe from storms," Katherine said. "She'll be all right. We'd better leave before the rain starts."

I was afraid the coming storm signaled the end to our discussion of Garth MacKay as Katherine seemed disinclined to say anything further. I planned to re-introduce the subject at a later time in another way.

"You'll like the Blue Lion Inn," she said. "It has a quaint medieval atmosphere, and the food is delicious. Nothing fancy. Just steaks and old-fashioned home cooking."

She took a black umbrella from a stand near the door. "While we have lunch, I'll tell you the story of my house. It has a fascinating history."

~ * ~

Katherine was right about the medieval ambiance of the Blue Lion Inn. It was a study in red with fanciful decorations marching parade-style in a border that wrapped around the walls. Knights from a long-past era, ladies in bright colored gowns and wimples, unicorns, some with wings, some without, and the blue lion himself, adorned with a wreath of red roses.

While a hostess dressed like a Chaucerian pilgrim greeted Katherine as if she were an old friend, I studied the illustrations. Each one seemed slightly different from its fellows. Take the unicorn closest to me, for instance. Surely his right wing was set at a higher angle than the one that followed him in the parade. And wasn't his horn a bit longer? And the blue lion beside him...had he just winked at me?

Anyone would think I had ingested a hallucinogen, but I hadn't had anything to eat and only a few sips of water from Katherine's pitcher.

It's the dim lighting, I told myself. *It makes the pictures look alarmingly realistic. Add a good measure of imagination, and you have living figures trapped in a wall.*

The hostess led us to a nook with a window view of Main Street, and even before we were comfortably settled, a waitress appeared with water and menus.

I was seated within touching space of a blue lion. He looked sad. For a moment, I thought I saw a tear stream down his face.

Good grief, Jennet, get a grip.

Sue closed her menu. "The vegetable beef soup sounds good."

"It has big chunks of beef in it, enough for a whole meal. I'll have a bowl, too."

"Tell us about your house, Katherine," Sue said. "You mentioned once that it was haunted but didn't go into detail. Jennet has an affinity for haunted houses."

Katherine looked at me and smiled. "Is that so? You would have loved mine. Right from the beginning, I knew I was out of my depth. Weird sounds like scratchings in the attic, a feeling that I wasn't alone, a ghostly voice. Things like that."

"So you set out to investigate?" I asked.

She nodded. "It turned out that a secret murderer lived in my perfect American town. His victim was, in a sense, my roommate. After I solved the mystery, the spirit was at peace, and things have been quiet ever since. Not so much as a shadow out of place."

"How did you discover who the killer was?" I asked.

But I had lost Katherine's attention. A group of five men stood inside the door. It was as if they had brought a burst of energy inside. With their entrance, the ambience shifted subtly. They weren't particularly boisterous, but it appeared that everyone in the Inn was aware of them. Was it my imagination or did the normal conversational hum of diners drop several decibels?

"Oh, no," Katherine murmured. "What appalling luck."

Our table was off the beaten path, so to speak, but the most striking of the newcomers, a brawny man with a neatly trimmed black beard, scanned the room, his gaze coming to rest on us. More accurately, on Katherine.

In the sudden silence, I heard the bearded man say, "You guys get a table. I'll be right with you." Whereupon, he headed toward us, his eyes fixed resolutely on Katherine. Ignoring Sue and me, he rested his hand on Sue's closed menu. He wore an unusual ring. It was a large silver lion's head with black stones for the eyes and sparkling diamonds in the mouth.

"Hello, Katherine," he said. "How have you been?"

"Well enough."

"Is school out?"

"Yes."

"That's good. What are you going to do this summer?"

She hesitated. "I'm taking a history course for another master's. I'm going to be busy reading and writing a paper."

"You're not taking a vacation?"

"I won't have time."

"Won't you have any downtime?"

"No."

He waited.

"There's the upkeep of the house and everything," she added.

"And everything," he echoed, a trace of mockery in his tone. "If you stay in town, maybe I'll see you around."

"Maybe."

He removed his hand from the menu and strode toward a table where his friends were in the process of placing their orders.

When he was out of earshot, Katherine said, "As you may have guessed, that was Garth MacKay."

"What a handsome man!" Sue noted.

And a dangerous one, I thought. *You can tell just by looking at him. Oh, yes, he could be a militiaman.*

"He still seems interested in you," Sue said.

Katherine opened her menu again, although she'd already made her selection. "We've both moved on."

So Garth was back in Maple Creek. Did that mean Ellalyn had returned to her house in Foxglove Corners? And where did Garth's obvious interest in rekindling his relationship with Katherine leave Ellalyn?

Twenty-nine

By the time we finished our lunch and thanked Katherine for her help, such as it was, the storm had moved east, leaving rain-soaked maple leaves to sparkle in the weak sunshine. Our picture-perfect summer day was back.

"What do you think?" Sue asked as I drove away from Walnut Street.

"That Garth MacKay is a member of the Michigan Militia and Katherine knows more about him than she said. I suspect the lady protested too much." I added, "I'm going to see if Ellalyn is back home. Zara might have been wrong about her being with her boyfriend."

"It's so hard knowing which way to turn when people aren't truthful," Sue said.

We passed the title house on the way out of town. The place looked deserted, the driveway empty. I wondered if Garth would keep the appointment Taryn had made for me, and if he would remember me from today's encounter. That was unlikely, as he'd hardly glanced at Sue and me.

Darn! I had to come up with some questions for Garth quickly, along with a reason for consulting him.

"I don't think I could walk away from a man like that," Sue said.

"You don't know him or anything about Katherine's relationship with him," I pointed out.

"True."

"What I think is that in some way the Michigan Militia is mixed up in this affair," I said.

"How?"

"I haven't figured that out."

"Katherine said it doesn't exist," Sue said.

"She's wrong. I need more facts. As it stands, I'm running around in circles, going nowhere."

"And Rainbow is still missing."

"And the person who should care the most is missing, too."

Or had Ellalyn come home?

This mystery may go deeper than you thought, I told myself.

"On the way home, let's drive by Ellalyn's house," I said. "Maybe she's there with Rainbow and there isn't a mystery after all."

~ * ~

She wasn't. Ellalyn's house had the closed, secretive look of Sky and MacKay Title. The grass was a few inches higher than it had been on our last drive-by, and bright yellow dandelions ran rampant in the lawn. Mail spilled out of the box onto the porch, Ellalyn's invitation to burglars as clear as the unkempt curbside view.

"If MacKay is having lunch at the Blue Lion Inn, I guess Ellalyn wasn't on vacation with him," Sue said.

"It doesn't look that way."

"So you're back in Square One. No dog. No Ellalyn."

"I'm not giving up," I said.

"With no good leads, what are you going to do?"

"Infiltrate the Michigan Militia."

"Seriously, Jennet. You'd never..."

"No, Crane would kill me. More accurately, I'm going to track them down. Brent will help me. I think."

"Then what?"

"Then I'll plan my next move."

My idea might be far-fetched, but I couldn't help thinking it was a source as yet untapped.

~ * ~

I found Brent at his barn playing ball with his collie pack, which was almost as large as mine. He looked every inch the countryman in a camel vest over a hunter green shirt and high boots. The sun, which had grown stronger by the hour, gave his dark red hair a fiery shine.

I made my way to the side of the barn, the pack gathering around me. Many of Brent's dogs were rescues. All knew and remembered me, especially Nova, the collie he had adopted last Christmas.

His voice boomed out in the deep silence. "What brings you out my way, Jennet?"

"A pet project of mine. Is there a place where can talk privately?"

"Sure. My office. I'm due for a coffee break."

Inside the barn, the fragrance of hay mixed pleasantly with the smells of horse and leather. Brent's first collie, Chance, and Nova followed us inside and lay at Brent's feet. As he fussed with the coffeemaker, I told him about my meeting with Garth MacKay and my impressions, which were, I had to admit, on the wild side.

"This MacKay sounds like a good man to stay away from," he said with a frown. "Tell me that your pet project doesn't involve him."

"In a way, it does. Do you remember the farmhouse you saw when you got lost coming home from Maple Falls, the place with all the shooting?"

"I don't get lost," he said. "I just took a wrong turn. But yes, I remember."

"Can you take me there?"

"Why?"

"I want to see it for myself."

"I repeat. Why?"

"Because of a hunch. Rainbow is Ellalyn's dog. Ellalyn has a connection of some sort to Garth MacKay. I believe he's a member of the Michigan Militia, or at least he supports it."

Brent brought two mugs down from a log shelf and wiped them with a dish towel. "Crane wouldn't want you to do this."

"I'm sure he wouldn't, but don't worry. I'll tell him after the fact." As Brent's frown deepened and he didn't respond, I added, "We don't even have to get out of the car. We'll pretend we took a wrong turn on the way to Foxglove Corners. Like you did."

"If we stay in the car, what do you expect to find out?

"I'll know when I see it," I said.

He cleared a space on the desk, shoving papers close to the edge.

"Lucy Hazen has hunches," he said.

"So do I. I've learned to pay attention to them from her."

"Why don't you ask her to look into her crystal ball?" Brent asked. "It'll be easier than going on a wild goose chase, and risk-free to boot."

"I may do that, too," I said. "So, are you in?"

"Against my better judgment. And you'd better not get me in trouble with the sheriff."

"It'll be perfectly safe," I promised.

I sort of believed that. Not entirely. The image of Garth MacKay formed in my mind...a burly, black-bearded figure dressed in unrelieved black with a gun belt strapped to his waist. A dangerous man, confident of his ability to sway others to his way of thinking.

"When can we go?" I asked.

Thirty

Annica set a lime cooler in front of me and one for herself. "These drinks should drop the temperature back to eighty."

Feeling as if I were half melted in the intense June heat, I took a sip of my drink, then another longer one. Annica's own invention, the lime cooler, was the essence of summer: minty, limey, fresh, and sweet. She had used taller glasses, usually reserved for iced tea, giving us another few delicious ounces to drink.

I had repeatedly asked her for the recipe, but she refused to part with it.

"It's my signature drink," she would say. "My secret. You have to come to Clovers to have one."

Well, I understood that, but I shared my mystery-based secrets with her.

Motioning to Marcy, her fellow waitress, to cover for her, Annica sat opposite me and unwrapped her straw. "Can I go with you to the militia place?"

I was anticipating this request. Annica always wanted to be included in my sleuthing.

"Sure, but as you can imagine, Brent isn't keen on the idea."

"Why? It sounds like a good one to me."

"The usual reason. He thinks it's dangerous, but we won't even get out of the car."

"Then nothing will happen." She stirred the frothy green liquid with her straw. "Will it?"

"I don't see how it could," I said, adding, "I never dreamed that the search for Rainbow would lead to the Michigan Militia. But it's possible I've strayed out into left field."

"We'll see. Speaking of Rainbow, weren't we supposed to go back to Woodsboro Park some day?"

I nodded. "I've put it off. Other things have happened."

In fact, I hadn't thought about the park much lately, but I'd dreamed about it. More than once, in fact. I was lost in an encroaching forest, trying to find my way to the people I'd come with. Or something like that. All I remembered was that my surroundings were dark and frightening, nightmare stuff, and I kept stepping off the path.

"Let's go this week," she said. "I have a light schedule. We can pack a lunch, and you can bring a couple of the dogs along. It'll be fun."

"Misty. She's the one with the special talent."

"Mmm. She's been at the park before and didn't sound the alert when Rainbow was taken."

"No. Her powers were off duty that day. But the third time may be the charm."

And perhaps giving voice to that sentiment would make it come true.

~ * ~

Brent's prized vintage Plymouth Belvedere sailed across the uneven country by-roads like a green-finned white bird. He had turned the air conditioning off and opened the windows. My hair was a tangled mess, but the air was hot and sweet; and I felt light and free.

He scowled at a nearby fork in the road. "It's weird approaching the farmhouse from Foxglove Corners. I'm getting confused."

"It's a nice day for a drive," Annica said. "We could head up to Maple Falls and look for it on the way back south."

"There has to be an easier way."

"What's the name of the road we're looking for?" I asked.

"I don't know. I didn't see a sign."

We had passed innumerable stretches of woods and lakes, tiny towns, sprawling farms, and horses gazing behind three-board plank fences. Then more woods and now the fork.

He brought the car to a stop. "Which way?"

"The road less traveled by," Annica said.

"Turn right," I countered. "We can always backtrack if it looks wrong."

"I don't remember any of this," Brent said.

He drove slowly, turning his head first right, then left, until we came to a red and white windmill standing sentinel over a barn in the background. No other structures were in sight. If there were a house on the property, it was well hidden behind a stand of tall fir trees.

He pulled the car to the side, even though the Plymouth was the only vehicle on the road.

"I remember this. I wondered if it was a real windmill or just ornamental."

Whichever it was, no one had taken the trouble to maintain it. The paint was peeling, and the pond it overlooked had a layer of leaves from past autumns covering water that was likely stagnant.

"So you wondered about the windmill," I said. "What did you do then?"

"I drove on about a half mile till I saw a row of small cottages. Summer places, I thought. I didn't see any people around. Then I heard shooting in the distance. Not just one shot. Lots of gunfire. Where the road ended, I saw an old white farmhouse with trucks parked in front."

"And?" Annica said.

"I wasn't about to stop and investigate. I turned around, kept driving, and eventually found the road to take me home."

I had forgotten about Brent's passenger, the tricolor collie who wasn't Rainbow.

"How did the dog react?" I asked.

"She was cowering in the back. It was too noisy for her."

"I don't hear any gunfire today," Annica said.

"That's good."

"Wait till we get closer," Brent said.

But the country peace and quiet prevailed, even as we spied a white farmhouse, a lone structure rising against an azure sky. It had clean, classic lines and a touch of gingerbread trim, but, like the windmill, it showed signs of neglect. Even from the car, I could see that it needed a fresh coat of paint, and one of the posts had fallen forward on the porch.

Brent's words had strengthened my suspicion that this isolated place was a stronghold where the men (and women?) of the Michigan Militia gathered to practice their shooting.

As we neared the house, he brought the car to a stop. "It doesn't look like anyone's home."

"Great!" Annica opened the door. "Then we can explore."

Thirty-one

"Annica!" I cried. "Come back.

Brent threw open his door and followed her. "That girl will be the death of me."

Unwilling to be separated from my companions, I joined Brent on what passed for the front yard, a jumble of weeds in an expanse of high grass, the whole overgrown with dandelions. Annica was on the porch peering into the farmhouse window, rubbing a larger space on a dusty pane.

"It's furnished," she said. "Someone lives here."

Or had lived there. The place had the distinct feel of a house long abandoned.

It didn't conform to my idea of a militia stronghold. A grand piano complete with open sheet music dominated the living room. About a half dozen framed photographs adorned the mantel, and an empty rocking chair sat close to the window.

The rocking chair seemed to move slightly. Certainly an illusion caused by sunshine filtered through a smudged window. I looked again and it was still.

The room looked innocuous enough, except for the two shotguns that claimed pride of place above the fireplace.

"Nobody's here now," Brent said. "Let's get out before someone shows up." He trained his eyes on me. "Just in case you were figuring on trying the door—Jennet."

I wasn't, but why not? I turned the doorknob. Locked, of course.

"Let's go around to the back," I said. "Isn't that where you heard the shooting?"

He glanced at the road. "Okay, but let's be quick."

He led the way to the back of the farmhouse, which appeared as derelict as the front. Only there the grasses and dandelions were trampled down. An empty doghouse with a chain attached lent a subtle air of despair to the scene. The land sloped downward, flowing into a wavy line of dark woods.

"They kept a dog chained up," I said. "I wonder where he is."

Brent shrugged. "Gone, like everybody else."

Everything that might point to a shooting field had been cleared away, although right at my foot, an object glinted from a clump of crabgrass. I picked it up and recoiled from the damp crusted mud that seemed to transfer itself to my hand.

"What did you find, Jennet?" Brent asked.

"An old-fashioned pocket watch on a chain. You don't see these around anymore."

I pulled a tissue from my pocket and wiped it clean. It was a handsome piece, the hands frozen on three-twenty. I looked for an inscription. There was none.

"What are you going to do with it?" Annica asked.

"Take it along."

"That's stealing," Brent said.

"It's a clue. The owner shouldn't have been so careless with it."

"Finders keepers," Annica added.

"All right," Brent said. "We've seen everything there is to see. Let's get out of here."

Annica took a few steps toward the woods, her eyes on the ground. "Maybe there's something else we can find."

"Now! I'm leaving with or without my passengers."

"You're no fun, Brent," Annica said.

But she came. I was the one who lingered.

I had a clue now, but, unfortunately, no idea what to do with it. The watch could have lain in the untended grass for ages; it could belong to anyone. But in case one of the militiamen had lost it...what? Would he return to the farm hoping to find it? How would I know? And how would keeping it benefit me?

Should I drop it back into the weeds and forget about it? Brent was opening the car door, and Annica had caught up to him. Brent would never drive away and leave me at the farmhouse. He wouldn't dare, but he was in a rare testy mood. I'd better not keep him waiting.

"Jennet!" he called. "Are you coming or did you find something else?"

Hastily, I dropped the watch into my pocket, resolving to think about it later.

~ * ~

When we had passed the cottages on the way to the farmhouse, we hadn't seen anybody or any sign of activity. Now, in front of a yellow cottage two young men were lifting a red canoe to a pair of sawhorses. A paint can and various related equipment surrounded them.

Brent brought the car to a stop and rolled down the window. The men set the canoe in place and strolled over to us, their eyes gleaming with admiration as they let their eyes rove over the vintage Belvedere.

They were both tall and blond and resembled each other. One was hefty, the other on the thin side. The hefty one had the name 'Chet' sewed onto the pocket of his denim shirt.

"Nice ride," Chet said. "Did it come like that?"

"You mean with the green fins? I had it custom painted."

"It looks like you just drove it off the lot."

"I restored it myself," Brent said.

The thin man extended his hand. "Name's Claud. Where'd you get the white walls?"

"Off another car." Claud let his hand caress the steering wheel. "Do you know the name of the road we're on?"

"It's North Windmill," Claud said. "It's not much of a road, but we like it here. You can walk to the lake."

"Do you know who lives in that white house down the road?" I asked.

Chet said, "No one since Gran Counselman passed, but her nephew uses the place on Saturdays for his parties."

"I'm in the market for a house in the country," I said.

Well, I was, once.

"And I was supposed to meet a friend here," Brent added. "I don't know if I have the right place."

"This used to be a nice, quiet area," Chet said. "Now it's like the Fourth of July every Saturday."

"Firecrackers?" I asked.

"Guns," he said. "Noisemakers. Scares the dogs out of a year's growth. We'd like to run those yokels out of town, but..." he shrugged. "What can you do? Complain, but no one does anything."

"That's wrong," I said.

Chet cast a baleful road in the direction of the farmhouse. "That's life."

~ * ~

We stopped for a cold drink at a small diner on the way home, an occasion that turned into a club sandwich break for Brent.

"What do you think?" he asked as he spread dill pickles on top of the bacon.

"That the farmhouse is suspicious, as I thought," I said.

"We have to go back some Saturday," Annica added.

Brent favored her with one of his most ferocious frowns. "We definitely do not."

"I'll tell Crane about it," I said. "Just in case it's what I think it is. He'll want to keep an eye on it."

"I guess there's no law against playing war games in the country," Annica said. "Unless you're traumatizing dogs and veterans with PTSD or people who like it quiet."

"Their neighbors shouldn't have to put up with all the disruption. I'm glad I live on Jonquil Lane."

Annica tasted her lemonade and stirred a teaspoon of sugar into it. "The purpose of a group like the Michigan Militia eludes me. What exactly is it they do? Or hope to do?"

"Take down the government," Brent said. "Fat chance of that."

While he demolished his sandwich, I sipped my drink, and pondered his words.

I agreed with him. I was proud of my country and had faith in our elected officials and dedicated law enforcers who would honor their oaths even unto death. Like Crane. They would keep us safe from dangerous groups like the Michigan Militia.

We *were* safe, weren't we?

Thirty-two

For our afternoon in the park, Annica brought sandwiches and cake from Clovers, and I supplied iced tea and Misty, with instructions to my talented white collie to turn on her red alert powers.

Not that I had high hopes for our excursion. We were simply taking advantage of another glorious summer day.

Still, a vague whisper slipped into my mind. I had found one clue, the pocket watch, in an unlikely place. Maybe I'd find another, an object dropped by Rainbow's abductor that would lead me to that despicable excuse for a human.

And maybe...roll back the years. With Misty's help, I might find evidence of what had happened to Celia Loring so long ago.

Don't count on it, I told myself. *Just enjoy sunshine and good company.*

But what gave birth to these wildly improbable developments?

Weakling optimism, I thought. *Harmless fantasy. Hope everlasting.*

Annica was tapping one of the charms on her bracelet with a frosty pink fingernail. It was a miniature gold ring. She was as restless as the strands of red-gold hair blowing free from her ponytail, as was Misty.

We'd chosen a bench close to the swings. As I watched a little girl in a yellow star-studded top soar high in the air, I wished I could take her place and see the park from a different perspective. Perhaps see back through the years. Was there a law against adults using the swings?

A familiar melody broke through my musings. The ice cream truck that apparently knew only one tune, "The Arkansas Traveler." Immediately, the girl brought the swing to a stop and joined the race to the park entrance in search of a frosty treat.

Misty whined and tugged on her leash, desperate to go with them.

The scene reminded me of the Pied Piper, playing his magic notes, summoning the town's children, leading them away. In my mind, I could almost see Celia Loring among the crowd of running children.

But what happened then?

"Let's walk over to the gazebo," Annica said. "I want to see if it's finished yet."

"Good idea."

Last week the *Banner* had printed an artist's rendering of the park's newest feature. A Victorian design, it would be encased by climbing red roses and was in easy walking distance of Woodsboro Lake. My only regret was the loss of the trees chopped down to clear the building site.

But the park had a wealth of trees, dark woods perfect for hiking and perhaps hiding.

A handmade sign tacked to an oak tree pointed us toward the gazebo. To my surprise, it was finished, building debris carted away, white paint gleaming in the sun. Inside, benches wrapped around the gazebo, and the bed around the base was raked and ready for planting. In bloom, the climbing roses would serve as curtains.

"That was fast," I said.

"This will be a nice place to sit and read," Annica said. "Or a nice place for lovers."

"For lovers? I wouldn't say so. It's too public."

"Well, nobody is here now."

Annica pulled out her phone and snapped a picture of the gazebo. Misty was sniffing at the freshly turned earth, clearly agitated.

Suddenly, she began to dig, sending dirt flying into the air. My pretty white collie. Her legs were rapidly acquiring a layer of dirt.

With visions of a bath and grooming session in the future, I said, "She loves to dig. All this loose dirt is too much of a temptation for her."

"She's doing damage. The gardeners will kill her."

"Not true. They can just set a rosebush in the hole. She's saving them time and effort."

Misty showed no sign of losing interest in her excavation. But if the park ranger were to see her...

"Misty, stop!" I said.

She ignored me, and to my dismay shoved her nose deep into her hole, only to emerge with a small object dangling from her mouth.

I tugged her back to my side. Freed from its burial place, the object caught the light of the sun.

Deja vu. Another pocket watch? Too small.

She dropped it, but whimpered anxiously as I examined her find. It was a tiny gold cross on a short, fine chain with the tiniest bit of sparkle at its center. A diamond chip?

I imagined a child suddenly realizing her cross was missing. Searching in vain, perhaps crying, not knowing that the earth had swallowed it where it would stay until Misty, super digger, with a little help from the park gardeners, resurrected it.

Something was wrong with this scenario, though. Annica and I realized it at the same time.

"This was all woods before they cleared the land to build the gazebo," I said. "Which means whoever lost this cross was in the woods. Exploring? Running for her life? We can't know, but she was here."

"This is your time for finding things, Jennet," Annica said. "It has to be valuable. Let's turn it over to the park ranger."

"No."

My mind had already made a giant leap to Celia. Could the cross have belonged to her? Could it be a clue to her fate? I had given Misty her orders. She had delivered.

Of course, it could have belonged to any little girl at any time over the past several years. Once lost in the woods, an object like this might as well have fallen into a black hole.

Well, in a way, it did.

I took a picture of the cross and slipped it into my pocket. "I'm giving it to the police," I said.

~ * ~

Our friend, Mac Dalby, had a passion for taking cold cases out of the proverbial deep freeze in the hope of stumbling across a clue that had somehow escaped everyone else's notice. He was even writing a book on the subject.

"It's my hobby," he once said. "More challenging than any puzzle."

To my knowledge, he had never solved one of these old mysteries. I figured he might be willing to accept the one I offered him.

While waiting for Crane to come home, I reflected on the strangest aspect of Misty's discovery. I'd wondered if I might find a clue at the park. Then Misty had come through for me.

It had happened, just as I'd visualized it, which was gratifying, but also weird and a trifle frightening. Wish for something and it's summarily granted. Did life work that way?

Later, Crane was quick to bring me back down to earth. After a teasing comment, "It's magic," he said, "I'm not surprised, Jennet. You've often said that everything goes back to Woodsboro Park."

"I was talking about Rainbow's abduction," I said.

"That, too."

"I'm going to try Mac again," I said, not counting on his eventual response to my voice mail.

This time he answered. "Jennet. How's everything on Jonquil Lane? Peaceful, I hope."

"Very. Do you remember the disappearance of a little girl named Celia Loring twenty years ago at Woodsboro Park?"

"Celia Loring," he said. "Seven years old. Vanished during an afternoon at the park while in the company of her aunt, Joanne Linder. Ms. Linder questioned. Several tips. None panned out. Why are you asking?"

"And do you remember the collie who was snatched from her crate at the Collie Walkabout?"

"Which was held at Woodsboro Park. Yes, she's still missing. That place has a reputation."

He proceeded to tell me about the boy who had drowned in the fountain, after which I described Misty's discovery.

"You're not saying there's a connection, are you?" he asked. "How could there be? The Loring case is practically ancient history."

"There could be. Twenty years isn't ancient history."

"That cross could have belonged to any child," he pointed out. "It's not something you see a modern kid wearing."

"I've told myself that, but there's a slim chance it could have belonged to Celia. Don't you think it's worth looking into?"

He paused while I braced myself for one of his typical condescending comments, perhaps one combining the words 'girl' and 'detective.' But finally he said, "I do. I'll have to look up the description of what the Loring girl was wearing when she disappeared. Where's the cross now?"

"With me. I'm looking at it."

The cross lay in my left palm, its tiny diamond chip glittering in the light of the study lamp. A diamond chip for a very young girl.

"I know an easier way to find out what Celia was wearing," I said. "Her aunt would know."

"If she remembers."

"She will."

In fact, she'd already told me. A pink sundress Joanne had made herself.

Thirty-three

"I gave Celia a cross when she made her first holy communion," Joanne said. "My uncle gave it to me when I was Celia's age. Celia wore it every day, even to play."

Joanne stared out the window, perhaps seeing Celia on her tricycle, Celia with her favorite plush animal in her arms, Celia with the diamond chip in her cross glittering in the sunlight of a summer long past.

"She was wearing it that day," Joanne said. "I wish I could see it. Then I'd know for certain."

I showed her the picture I'd taken.

"It looks like Celia's cross, but I want to hold it in my hand."

"Mac Dalby will keep it safe and eventually return it to you."

In my heart, I knew the cross had once belonged to Celia. I didn't need proof. As to how she had lost it...we didn't speculate.

"I have to call my sister," Joanne said.

"Maybe you should wait until you actually see the cross."

"We've already waited twenty years. What will happen now?"

"Mac didn't say, but I assume they'll search the area thoroughly."

Looking for a body. No, for bones. A child's skeleton.

"They can't dig up the whole park," Joanne said.

"No, but that soon-to-be flower bed is a starting point. Celia could have been passing through when she lost the cross."

"Twenty years ago that area was deep woods."

"Here's another possibility," I said. "The clasp broke and fell, Celia didn't notice it, but a bird did. That bird carried it away."

Joanne nodded. "Birds do that."

A mental picture of a hovering vulture sent a chill cascading over me. I shoved it away.

"If I were in charge of the search, I'd concentrate on the land around the gazebo," I said.

Tears glistened in Joanne's eyes. Impatiently, she wiped them away. "I may have to abandon my idea of finding Celia alive and grown with a story to explain where she's been all these years. I want to be part of the search, Jennet."

"I'm sure Mac will allow that."

Joanne was quiet for a long time, obviously struggling to keep her tears at bay.

Finally, she murmured, "She's been so long at the park."

"Twenty years," I said.

~ * ~

Misty was restless. In my haste to give the dogs fresh water and biscuits and let them play in the fresh air, I didn't notice it at first.

While Star and Halley play-fought over the communal red Frisbee, Misty paced, going as far to Jonquil Lane as she dared.

All of the collies had been trained to stay away from the road. She was too close to the edge. I called her, but she only turned to look at me.

What now?

Call her again.

She came and nudged my knee, whimpering, going so far as to grab the hem of my long denim skirt in her mouth.

Lassie leading Timmy to the victim bound and gagged in the barn?

"What's wrong, girl?"

Her whimpering took on a desperate tone, almost a screech.

"Misty?"

Could she possibly want to go back to Woodsboro Park to keep digging? I had dragged her away from her precious hole, all of my attention on the gold cross.

"We'll go tomorrow," I said.

I had planned a second trip to the park anyway. I wanted to see if Mac was going to act on the information I'd given him and if Joanne was at the park. I felt certain she was.

I had claimed this mystery for my own and had no intention of waiting for news at home.

Later, as he locked his gun in the cabinet, Crane noticed Misty's anxiety, her continued pacing and whining.

"Is she feeling all right?" he asked as she refused a choice piece of beef at dinner.

"I don't think it's physical," I said.

"But we don't know. You'd better take her to the vet if she doesn't settle down."

"I could, but the vet won't find anything wrong with her."

Vets didn't have all the answers. Doctor Foster wouldn't know about the cross unless I told her.

I told Crane what I suspected. "I'll take her back to the park in the morning instead," I said.

Still later that evening, Mac Dalby called. I never thought we'd be on the same wavelength, so I was surprised when he said, "I'd like to borrow your white collie."

I said the first thing that came to my mind. "She isn't a cadaver dog."

"That's okay. We're not looking for a cadaver."

"Can't you search without Misty?"

"Our task is overwhelming. You've often bragged about Misty's talents. She might be able to help us—find something else."

"I'll bring her to the park tomorrow," I said and dropped the phone back into my purse.

Misty had followed me to the kitchen. It was as if she knew the call concerned her.

She does, I thought.

Thirty-four

As I stood on the fringe of the crowd that had gathered to watch the search at the gazebo, the sun beat down on my bare head. My hair felt as if it were on fire. The silk blouse I'd donned that morning, thinking it would keep me cool, was wrinkled and damp.

Joanne stood beside me fanning herself with what appeared to be a large prayer card. "I'm so nervous," she said. Then, "It's so ungodly hot."

Unmindful of the temperature, which must be at least ninety, Misty dug away, tearing apart the ground about three yards from the future flower beds. This was what she had been wanting since I'd taken her away from her hole.

She knows.

A young girl stepped in front of me, taking pictures with her phone. "I didn't know the force had a canine officer," she said.

I couldn't resist commenting, although she had addressed her companion. "They don't. She's mine."

"Isn't she amazing?" the girl asked. "Did you train her to find stuff?"

I thought back to the evening of Misty's coming. The Christmas Eve snowstorm. The abandoned white puppy on my porch. Her gradually revealed talents.

"No, it comes naturally to her." I didn't specify what "it" was. "If there's anything to find, my Misty will find it."

"Over here!" Mac called out. "We got something."

In the sudden silence, he pulled Misty back from her new hole. I took her leash, whispering, "Good girl, Misty. You did it."

Ignoring the uniformed guards appointed to hold back the crowd, I made my way to Mac's side. "What did you find?" I asked.

"An arm. A small arm."

A child's arm. As the rest of the skeleton revealed itself, the hush that had descended over the park erupted into a barrage of questions.

Is it real?

Who is it?

How did the dog know it was there?

It? No, she. I didn't need official confirmation. I had no doubt I was looking at the remains of Celia Loring, found at last.

So long at the park, I thought.

"Hey, someone help her!"

The shouted command brought me back to my surroundings.

Joanne had slumped to the ground, still clutching the prayer card-fan. She was conscious. Her eyes were open, but she looked like a rag doll that has lost its stuffing.

"Is she all right?" someone demanded.

Another voice added in. "It's the heat. It must be a hundred in the shade."

The girl who had admired Misty was holding a bottle of water in front of Joanne's mouth. "Let me help you over to the shade," she said.

"No. I'm okay." She stood beside me, unsteady, but resolute. "It's Celia, isn't it?"

The police would need concrete identification. They had ways of doing that, even after all the time that had passed. All I needed was the size of the bones and the location of the burial place, near the cross. And Misty's incredible intuition.

"It must be," I said. "I'm so sorry, Joanne."

"She never grew up. She was always here. I always suspected she never left the park. But what happened to her? What monster did this to her?"

She looked into Misty's eyes. "Can you help me find out, girl?"

"She can't do that," I said quickly.

~ * ~

But Misty, the Wonder Dog, could do anything. That was the opinion of the reporter who had recorded her achievement for canine posterity.

I sat in my favorite booth at Clovers the next morning with a pot of tea, a blueberry muffin, and the *Banner*, where a picture of my beautiful white collie graced the front page, along with a story of her amazing discovery.

Annica, who had taken her break, read a line, making no attempt to hide her delight. *A collie belonging to Foxglove Corners resident, Jennet Ferguson, does what the police have been unable to do.* I'll bet Mac Dalby won't be happy to read that."

"Mac is happy, period," I said. "He's gone back to the old case, determined to identify the killer."

I hadn't had a choice of keeping the story quiet. Among the crowd were reporters, including an old friend, Jill Lodge, from Maple Falls. How had the press learned of Misty 's exploits so quickly? As for Jill, had she flown in from Maple Falls?

But Misty deserved every accolade that came her way, the least of which was a front page spread which included a sidebar depicting her history with me. Her most appreciated reward, though, came in the form of two T-bone steaks large enough to feed eight collies and two owners.

Lurking in the back of my memory was the achievement of another collie, Winter, who had saved a child from drowning. Sadly, the publicity attending that event had come to the attention of an old enemy. Recalling the aftermath of that day, I pushed the memory as far down in my mind as it would go.

That wouldn't happen to Misty. I wouldn't let it.

"What are the odds the killer is still in the area?" Annica asked.

"Slight. Who murders and stays close to the crime scene?"

Some people, I thought, if they felt safe.

"Mac mentioned Celia's aunt was questioned," I said.

"Do you think she did it?"

Joanne, still heartsick at the loss of her beloved niece who had disappeared on her watch?

No, not Joanne.

"I'm sure everyone who knew Celia was interviewed at the time," I said. "Especially the people at the park, the ones who didn't scatter after it was apparent that Celia had vanished."

"Some of them may have moved out of the state or passed away."

"Mac said he's going to investigate every possible angle."

"Let me give you a word of advice," Annica said. "Stay well out of this investigation. Waay out."

"That's more than two words."

"Yeah, well, you get the message."

Annica didn't have to issue dire warnings. My part in the mystery was over. Still, her words set a definite chill wafting through the air. I remembered one of my grandmother's frequently uttered sayings: *A goose just walked over my grave.*

I felt that way then.

Thirty-five

The letters in the headline were gigantic, the kind of font usually reserved for momentous events like tornadoes or insurrections: *Michigan Man Arrested in Kidnap Plot*.

What now? Letting my tea cool, I read the story. Stories, I should say. Accompanied by two head shots, they had taken over the front page, pushing Misty's exploits into oblivion.

The face of the alleged kidnapper looked familiar. He had handsome features and light hair topped by a Stetson. A make-believe cowboy, he looked straight at the camera with a grim expression. He knew he was in deep trouble, but he would go down fighting, bluff his way through whatever fate threw at him. He was Gregory Sky of Maple Creek.

Sky and MacKay Title.

I remembered then. Gregory Sky was Garth MacKay's partner, a man I'd never seen. Then why was his face familiar?

Also pictured was his intended victim. She was Representative Justina Granville, young, charismatic, and eager to implement reforms wherever she saw the need.

I read on. Gregory Sky was a reputed member of the Michigan Militia. Of course, he denied any knowledge of the organization and the plan to abduct Representative Granville when she paid her annual visit to the Granville family home on the outskirts of Maple Creek.

For what purpose?

Ostensibly to force her to ban legislation intended to protect Maple Falls' wolf population, an accusation he vehemently denied. Justina Granville had a fondness for wildlife, especially wolves. She had established a shelter dedicated to rescuing wolves who had been kept as household pets, together with the occasional wolf-dog hybrid. According to the militia, if she didn't agree to support the legislation, they would see to it that she was summarily exterminated.

Exterminated was an odd word choice. Why not simply say 'killed'?

The plot sounded fantastic, the kind of story one would find in an old time series book. But apparently, according to the unnamed person who had betrayed Sky, it was real and had been in the planning stage for several months.

At present, Ms. Granville was in an undisclosed location, having escaped the fate planned for her. She had hired two bodyguards. Gregory Sky was in custody, the unidentified informer in hiding. As the investigation was ongoing, further arrests were imminent.

I found it hard to believe that people who objected to protection for the wolves were that passionate. And I wondered... I'd gotten word that Taryn MacKay had cancelled my appointment with Garth MacKay and said it would be impossible to reschedule it. Could there be a connection?

I refolded the paper and took a sip of tea, so cool it might as well be an iced beverage. "Well, Misty, this is weird."

She sat at my side, eyes bright with anticipation, no doubt hoping a new adventure was forthcoming. I glanced from her to Velvet, who lay in front of the stove chewing a bone, acting more like a normal dog. My Misty was anything but normal.

The phone rang. Brent's voice boomed out, "Hey, Jennet! Did you see the *Banner* this morning?"

"Just now," I said. "It's bizarre."

"It makes no sense. Save the wolves? It's a noble cause, but I don't think we're getting the full story."

"Probably not. It's just happening."

"I'm on my way to the farmhouse," he said.

"Why?"

"To see if anything's going on there. I still think it's a militia hangout."

"If so, that's a good reason to avoid the place. We should be heading the other way."

"That's no fun. Want to come along?"

I considered. The sun was shining, bathing the landscape in pure gold. Through the half-open kitchen window, the air blew fresh and floral-scented, promising another ideal summer day. The kind of day for an adventure.

"I would," I said, "but I wonder if it's safe."

"Annica has a class this morning. We won't leave the car. Promise. It'll be a quick drive-by. I don't think anyone's hanging around there."

It never takes much to tempt me. My morning was free; indeed, my entire day was a chapter waiting to be written. "It sounds harmless."

Misty placed her paw heavily on my lap as if to remind me that she, no less than Annica, was my partner-in-detection.

"I'll take Misty," I said.

"And I have Nova and Chance with me."

I glanced around the kitchen. Everything was stored away and gleaming. I had a roast thawing in the refrigerator and a chocolate cake on the counter.

"Give me a half hour to let the dogs out and get ready," I said.

~ * ~

When we reached the yellow cottage at which we'd stopped on our previous visit, Brent brought the Plymouth to a rolling stop. The canoe, painted bright red, rested on the sawhorses. The two men who had admired the vintage Belvedere sat on lawn chairs eating sandwiches and drinking beer. Cans, empty and unopened, littered the grass around them.

They sprang to life when they saw us.

The burly blond man, Chet, if I remembered right, had a wavy line of red paint on his cheek. He reached the car first and ran his hand lovingly over the long white fins. Nova growled, and Chance snapped in the general direction of the window. Chet ignored him.

"They sure knew how to make good looking cars in them days," Claud said.

Chet narrowed suspicious dark eyes. "What brings you guys to our neck of the woods—again?" he asked.

Brent hesitated, obviously not having a reason prepared.

"I'm still looking for property near a lake," I said. "I wanted to see that old farmhouse again."

"Like I told you, it's not for sale. Especially not now."

"What's different about now?" I asked.

"The plot to kidnap that rep lady."

"What plot?"

"It's in all the papers."

Claud said, "I always thought they were up to no good at that place. All that shooting. You don't want to buy a house with a bad reputation, miss."

I don't understand," I said. "What does the kidnap plot have to do with the farmhouse?"

"I seen the guy whose picture was in the paper there. I think he's the old lady's son or maybe her nephew."

In truth, I *did* see the connection. Son or nephew, militia hangout, kidnap plot. "Maybe the owner will want to unload it before everyone knows it's connected to a crime."

"We can look," Brent said. "No law against that."

"Do you know where I can get a car with fins?" Chet asked.

~ * ~

The farmhouse was the essence of desolation, a sad relic whose best days had long since passed. It sat in a wilderness of untended grass grown higher since the last time we'd seen it. Blowsy dandelions gave the picture a welcome splash of color.

"It needs a lot of work," Brent said.

"Well, I'm not really going to buy it."

My voice sounded strange to me. I should be used to country silence, but this silence had a different quality. It would have been at home in a graveyard.

"I thought there'd be yellow tape up," Brent said.

"It isn't a crime scene."

"But it was going to be. Weren't they planning to keep that lady politician here?"

"I don't remember reading that."

"It was on TV. The cops searched the place but didn't find anything much. Just a lot of dusty furniture and stacks of old newspapers. There were guns, but they weren't loaded. Just for decoration, I guess."

"The shooters probably stayed outside. Maybe they just went in to use the bathroom or kitchen. I wonder about the newspapers, though."

The rumble of a vehicle broke through the silence. A rusty blue truck sped down the road, sending gravel flying into the air and stirring up dust. It pulled up alongside the Plymouth, and the driver glared at us. He wouldn't know me, but I recognized him from my one sighting at the Blue Lion Inn. Garth MacKay, he of the black beard and mysterious background.

I saw instantly the attraction he must hold (have held?) for Ellalyn and before her, for Katherine Kale. In that moment, he stared at me, seeming to take my measure. I became aware of the goose walking over my grave sensation again.

Misty jumped across the seat and landed in my lap, barking furiously at the intruder as if this section of roadway was her turf.

Correction. We were the intruders.

I tried to shove her into the back seat, but she had other ideas. She clawed at the window, blocking my view with her body. Which was a good idea.

"We're out of here," Brent said and stepped down hard on the gas pedal.

Thirty-six

"If he follows us, I'll look for another way home," Brent said. "We'll throw him off the trail."

I pushed Misty to one side, closer to Brent, but she refused to move. The truck was still there. I didn't see Garth MacKay. Presumably he had gone inside, which suggested he was familiar with the place. Perhaps he had a key, or the door was unlocked.

Brent sped past the yellow house and turned left on the next road. "Maybe this wasn't the best idea I ever had," he said as he rounded a curve. "Oh, well, no harm done."

"Except that he saw me."

"Do you know who he was?" he asked.

"Garth MacKay. Suspected militiaman. Luckily the girl in the title office cancelled my appointment or he would have recognized me."

Except...my heart sank as I considered Misty. If Garth read the *Banner*—and why wouldn't he, with his partner arrested and accused of planning an abduction?—he would presumably know about Misty's discovery at Woodsboro Park. My name, as her owner, had been included in the accounts.

But not my picture. Still, if MacKay wanted to find me, it would be relatively easy, as I was certain I had the only tri-headed white collie in the county, one with a reputation for uncovering that which was to have remained hidden.

As I pointed this out to Brent, he said, "Nothing will come of it, trust me. And if by chance it does, we'll say we were out for an afternoon drive. Looking for a farmhouse to buy."

"And when a man who could have been the owner showed up, we took off? We need a better excuse."

"I'll admit it might turn out to be a problem if that guy is one of the militia types. He must be, if his partner is involved with them. You'd better not tell the sheriff about our little trip."

"I don't keep secrets from Crane," I said.

"Since when?"

"When I don't want him to worry unnecessarily."

At least that was what I told myself.

"Too bad Misty's white," he said after a moment.

We were driving through a long, wooded stretch with signs posted at frequent intervals to warn away hunters and trespassers. I always enjoyed looking at the spectacular scenery for which this part of the state was famous, but in this case, I didn't want us to get lost. Especially with three dogs in the car.

"Since MacKay isn't following us, shouldn't we go back the way we came?" I asked.

"I guess. If I can find it."

"Don't you have a map in the glove compartment?"

"Yeah. It's from 1959. Just for show. Things may have changed since then. But don't worry. We're bound to run into the right road sooner or later."

Mildly encouraged, I leaned back and watched the seemingly unending panorama slide by. Misty had gone to sleep, her head in my lap. I tried not to think about what Garth MacKay was doing back at the farmhouse.

On the way home, Brent offered to treat me to lunch. Thinking of the roast and considering that we had dogs with us, I invited him to dinner instead.

If, that is, he managed to find the road home.

~ * ~

He did, and I was as happy to see the house on Jonquil Lane as I'd been to set out on a new adventure earlier in the day.

When Crane learned about our near encounter with a militiaman, he turned frosty gray eyes on Brent. "You're leading my wife astray, Fowler. I order you to cease and desist. Luck was with you this time."

"It was my idea," I said. "Kind of." To defuse the situation, I added, "I wonder what MacKay was doing at the farmhouse."

"Destroying hidden evidence?" Brent said.

"Or maybe looking for his pocket watch? And I have it."

"You *still* have it?" Crane frowned. "I'll turn it in to Mac for you. Just in case this MacKay comes looking for it."

"He doesn't seem like the pocket watch kind," I said.

But there was his fancy lion's head ring with the black stones and diamonds. What did I know about men's fashion preferences? The pocket watch might be a treasured heirloom.

Well, I wouldn't go strolling through the back yard of the militia house again, with or without Brent.

In fact, I needed to step a few paces away from both mysteries and enjoy the beautiful summer weather. It wouldn't last forever.

~ * ~

The next morning, I invited myself to tea at Lucy Hazen's house, Dark Gables. Tea meant tea leaves. I can't say that I believed wholeheartedly in Lucy's ability to foretell future events in the formations, but I had faith in her occasional glimpses into a time yet to come.

Would Celia Loring's killer be found decades later? Would I ever know what had happened to Rainbow, or for that matter to Ellalyn? Perhaps Lucy could tell me. In any event, it was another in a string of pleasant summer days and I hadn't visited Lucy in a long time.

Something was bothering her.

She shooed Sky away from the coffee table as she poured boiling water into a new teapot decorated with images of the sun and the moon and stars. The gold Zodiac charms on her bracelet jingled merrily.

"I had a nightmare last night," she said. "I wonder if it's a portent of sorts."

"What did you dream about?" I asked.

"I was there at the park when Misty discovered Celia Loring. Only she wasn't a skeleton."

I ignored an inner shiver. Lucy's nightmare was like her books. Pure Gothic. But then, wasn't that true of any nightmare?

"What was she then?"

"Perfectly preserved. A little girl in a white dress with a gold cross on a chain around her neck."

"But that's impossible," I said. "Misty found the cross in another place before she discovered the grave."

"This was a dream, Jennet. You know how dreams work."

I knew my own. Images dredged up from a variety of sources, emotions, usually fear, no smooth transitions from one scene to another. A chaotic pattern that tended to dissipate as the body passed to a waking state.

Knowing this, I still couldn't stop myself from wondering about the white dress. When she disappeared, Celia was wearing play clothes, a pink sundress.

"She reminded me of Snow White," Lucy said. "Only asleep, not dead."

"There's no question the bones are Celia's," I said.

"No, of course not. But here's the important part of the dream. There was something evil in the park. I couldn't see it but sensed its presence. Then I was running through the woods. Then..." she paused to stroke Sky's head. "I woke up. Sky was barking at something. Probably a creature too near the house. What I take from the dream is that Evil has moved into Foxglove Corners. Again. It's more powerful than ever. My advice to you is to beware."

"Of what exactly?"

"I'm not sure."

Lucy's warnings were often unspecified, which weren't of much help to one who wished to stay safe.

"Of Celia's killer, do you suppose?"

"Possibly. When all is said and done, it was only a dream."

She reached for my teacup, which was primed and ready to shower me with happy news and wishes granted.

"I see a rainbow," she said, pointing to a formation that did indeed look like a graceful arc without the colors.

"But, as always, you have to live through the storm first," she added.

Thirty-seven

On a day when Annica didn't have a class or a shift at Clovers, she proposed we take a trip to Maple Creek to go antiquing. Like Leonora, she was always looking for the perfect lamp. Also, the pink Victorian of which she was enamored was holding an open house. Its asking price had been reduced by two thousand dollars.

Annica sounded like a serious buyer, not like a single girl who worked as a waitress to pay her college tuition. At least she could pass for one, and anyone could attend an open house.

"Maybe that title man will be back in his office and you can see him," she said.

"Garth MacKay. I don't *want* to see him." I told her about my near encounter with him at the farmhouse. "Brent is sure it's a militia hangout, and why else would he be there?"

"You and Brent went somewhere together? Why wasn't I invited?"

"You told Brent you had a class."

"Well, I don't want to miss out on any more action."

"Then you might have to skip a class here and there."

"I don't want to do that. What about Maple Creek? Would you like to go?"

I didn't understand Annica's fascination with that house, but the town had other attractions, among them the Lost in the Past Antique Shop. Again, the day was ideal for a summer excursion. Best of all, it would be safe.

"We can have lunch at that medieval place, the Blue Unicorn," she said.

"The Red Lion. That sounds like fun. A getaway, and we don't have to drive across the state."

So we set out on an expedition that had nothing to do with mystery.

When we passed the purple Victorian that housed Garth MacKay's title company, nothing indicated it was open for business, not even a car in the lot. I could barely make out a sign on the front door but not its message. 'Closed Until Further Notice' probably, or something similar. With one of the partners arrested, confidence in MacKay and Sky must have plummeted. But wasn't this supposed to be a mystery-free day?

Annica's eyes lit up as we approached the pink Victorian. Deep pink and white impatiens sparkled around the foundation and in huge planters on either side of the front door.

"It's so beautiful," she said.

"It certainly is."

The realtor who had walked out to meet us overheard Annica's comment. "I'm Allyson Miller. You won't find another house like this in Maple Creek."

I doubted that, as several similar Victorians occupied the entire block, but this was the only one painted pink.

"It looks like a strawberry cake trimmed with white frosting," Annica said.

"Mmm, yes. You could say that." Ms. Miller looked from Annica to me and back to Annica. "Which one of you is the buyer?"

"I am," Annica said. "I'm lining up properties for my husband to view."

Ever the actress, she spoke as if her husband were a reality. "We plan to start a family soon."

"This house has plenty of room for children. I'll let you see for yourself."

For the next hour, we toured the house, peering into empty rooms while Annica fantasized about how she would decorate them. "With a lot of pink to carry on the color scheme," she said.

She paused in a spacious dining room large enough to accommodate a dozen people around a long table. "If only we could move this house to Foxglove Corners."

"It could be done, but it'd be easier to build a similar one. Cheaper, too."

She frowned. "But then, it wouldn't be a genuine Victorian."

"You can't have everything, Annica," I pointed out.

She gave me a secretive smile. "Yes, I can."

Oh, to have the boundless confidence of the young.

"I'm getting hungry," she said. "Let's have lunch now. We can go shopping after."

That met with my approval. I'd only had a blueberry muffin and tea for breakfast with Crane, and that was hours ago.

"At the Red Unicorn," she said.

Except for pink, she persisted in getting her colors mixed up. "The Blue Lion," I said.

~ * ~

As soon as we entered the restaurant and drew the attention of the hostess, I saw Celia's aunt, Joanne, sitting in a booth with a friend. She looked up from the menu she'd been perusing with a wide smile.

"Jennet! What a coincidence! We were just talking about you."

The hostess came to a stop, waiting for us to move or not, whatever developed.

"Won't you join us?" Joanne asked.

"We'd love to."

With a smile, the hostess withdrew.

I slid onto the bench next to Joanne and glanced at the wall decor. Images of blue unicorns interspersed with medieval maids in blue and flowers in bold primary colors. They were acting like proper wall decorations today, not moving, not trying to convey secret messages.

"How have you been?" I asked.

"Okay, I guess. I'm a bit anxious now that there's something to look forward to. This is my friend, Marigold Asher."

The woman with the unusual flower name. I'd heard Joanne speak of her.

Their friendship had begun when Celia had vanished. Marigold had been at the park on that fateful day and had helped Joanne search for her niece. Ever since, Marigold had been a source of support for Joanne, and the two had remained close friends over the years.

In a nod to her name, Marigold's linen dress was bright tangerine, and she wore a matching shade of lipstick, which, in most cases, wouldn't flatter an older woman. She hadn't lost her dark brown hair either, although I suspected it was dyed.

As she waved her hands, I noticed her ring, a chunky turquoise stone in an ornate gold setting that provided a rich contrast for the explosion of orange. "This is the best restaurant in Maple Creek, bar none," Marigold said.

I nodded. "We've been here before."

"Did you come to Maple Creek to shop?" Joanne asked.

"That and other things," Annica's glance at me clearly said she didn't want to mention her dream house. I understood that.

"We're going to Lost in the Past," I said.

"They have some lovely antiques," Joanne said. "Stepping through the door is like taking a trip back in time."

Odd that she'd mention time travel. Perhaps not so odd, given the shop's name.

"That must be true of any antique shop," I said.

"I'm looking for one of those *Gone with the Wind* lamps, "Annica said. "It has to be pink with cabbage roses on the globes."

I said I collected old time books in a series, then before I forgot, added, "You said you were talking about me?"

"About your marvelous collie," Joanne said. "She's really like Lassie, isn't she? Thanks to her, now I believe there'll be justice for my Celia. I just have to be patient a little longer."

"Don't get your hopes up," Marigold said quickly. "It's been so long since it happened.

So long at the park, I thought.

"Is there any news?" I asked.

"None that I've heard. It's early days."

"Lieutenant Dalby is determined to find the killer, but he has other priorities," I pointed out.

"At least somebody is looking into my case," Joanne said.

Marigold gave a subtle scoff. "He won't find anything. Too many years have passed since Celia left us. People move. They die. The police didn't solve the mystery at the time. They didn't even know Celia was dead."

Joanne's voice trembled slightly. "I need to keep my hope alive, Marigold. Allow me to do that, please."

Marigold's answer seemed unnecessarily sharp. "Suit yourself, I suppose, but it's like looking for a snowball in hell."

She moved her ring around on her finger. It was obviously too large and must be uncomfortably heavy. I wished she didn't sound so sure of herself. You'd think she would show a modicum of encouragement for her friend. After all, hope was free.

"Lieutenant Dalby has a special interest in cold cases," I said. "He's like a dog with a favorite bone."

"He doesn't work miracles, does he?" Marigold asked.

"No, but he's perceptive and determined."

"Let's wish him luck then."

The words were right, but the tone appeared to suggest the opposite.

Mac and I had often tangled over the past, mostly over his condescension and my interference in what he regarded as police business, but for the first time in ages, I found myself rooting for him.

Thirty-eight

The high point of our day trip to Maple Creek was that Annica found her lamp. It might have been made to order for her, with pink and yellow roses splashed on rosy globes with fluted edges.

"Now all I need is the house to put it in," she said.

The house, I thought. Annica certainly knew what she wanted: the lamp, the house, the man.

"In the meantime, I'll keep it on my nightstand," she said.

The low point was a suspicious envelope in the day's mail. It contained a single sheet of notepaper with letters cut from a newspaper or magazine. The message was obscure. *Better safe then sorry.* Rusty's latest missive, no doubt.

Being an English teacher, I focused first on the misspelling, or rather the misuse. Then I sought to interpret the line. It didn't sound like a threat. Had he dipped into a thesaurus, looking for 'sorry' quotations without sorting them for relevance?

I told myself Rusty had been my student. Hadn't I taught him anything?

Quickly I leaped to my own defense. He didn't give me a chance as he had summarily opted out of my class.

Be that as it may, I hadn't thought about Rusty or Marston High School for weeks. Close encounters with the Michigan Militia had been of more immediate concern. But my disgruntled student was obviously still out there, still bent on revenge for my part in denying him the chance to graduate.

Still out there, with his scissors and paste and various usages of his favorite word.

I dropped the paper into a basket I kept for items to be dealt with later—or never.

~ * ~

Whenever I was out and about, I drove by Ellalyn Zoller's house on the off chance she would be home. This morning, a different sight greeted me. The porch had been swept clean, all spilled mail taken away.

Did this mean Ellalyn had returned? I didn't see a car and the drapes remained closed, effectively blocking the interior from prying eyes.

I rapped lightly on the door, then more loudly, realizing a neighbor could have gathered the mail. But why hadn't this neighbor done so before?

At that moment, I thought I heard a muffled sound beyond the door. Approaching footsteps? I held my breath and waited. Was that a whimper, hastily cut off?

If by some miracle, Rainbow had been found, I'd surely hear her barking, not crying. What dog wouldn't sound the alarm at the first signs of an intruder?

Finally, standing in a pool of silence, I had to admit there was no dog, and, if Ellalyn were inside, she didn't want company. I walked back to the curb and waited for a bright blue Tesla to pass before crossing the street.

Garth MacKay was back in town. Where was Ellalyn, if not hiding in her house?

Obviously, I wouldn't find out today.

~ * ~

Our string of warm summer days had left the parched earth practically crying out for rain. Even a brief shower would suffice. My garden needed constant watering, and still some plants insisted on drooping, especially my rocket hybrid snapdragons.

Camille moved through her gardens early in the mornings, adjusting the location of the sprinkler. Her flowers were radiant, the most impressive display on Jonquil Lane.

Mine were doing as well as they could with Misty frequently digging close to the roots of a plant, and sometimes yanking it out of the ground in her zeal. I supposed she thought one day she would find another cross or a cache of human bones.

From the depths of my shoulder bag came the notes of my cell phone. I pulled it out and saw Joanne Linder's name. It was only seven-thirty, rather early for a call, unless something had happened.

"Good morning, Jennet," she said. "I'd like to invite you to join us for a funeral on Friday."

"Who died?" I asked.

"It's for Celia. Her mother was able to buy a single plot, and I found a priest who'll conduct the services. Celia will be laid to rest in a cemetery close to you, on Huron Court."

I gave an involuntary shudder. That accursed road where an unsuspecting traveler could drive straight back into the past or simply cruise along a country lane. The transition happened in the beat of a heart and without a warning. Or it could choose to act like any ordinary road. I tried to avoid it.

But the cemetery was still consecrated ground, the final resting place of Violet Randall, who had lived on Huron Court, and, even more recently, of Holly Wickersham, the young writer who had disappeared during a tornado.

"I'll go," I said, but added to myself, "Not alone."

"I thought it would be small, but I'm amazed at the people who remember Celia and want to say goodbye to her," she said. "Mac has been asking questions in Maple Creek, which has stirred up some interest. Then there was the newspaper coverage. After the funeral, I thought I'd host a lunch at the Blue Lion."

"Rather than drive back to Maple Creek, why don't you invite people to come to my house for lunch?" I asked.

"Thank you, but I couldn't impose," she said.

"I'd love to do it. For Celia."

I would have to go to the grocery store for ham and other lunch meats, soft drinks, an assortment of summer fruits...

Did I really want to do this?

Yes. It would be a fitting tribute to a little girl whose disappearance and subsequent murder had wound themselves around the fabric of my life. And perhaps one of the mourners possessed knowledge that would help Mac solve his cold case.

You never know.

Thirty-nine

Having driven to the end of Huron Court without being whisked away to another time, I stood with Annica and Brent at the cemetery's newest grave and listened to the priest intone prayers for the repose of the soul of Celia Margaret Loring. They came twenty years after the fact but were still welcome.

I imagined Celia sitting on top of a low-lying cloud, wanting to comfort her mother and her aunt, but unable to do it.

The humid air made it difficult to breathe, but at least I'd had the forethought to wear a shrug over my black linen dress to protect my arms from the burning sun. Never comfortable at a burial, I gazed at the distant shade trees with longing.

Eternal rest grant unto her, O Lord, and let perpetual light shine upon her...

It had been dark in Celia's makeshift grave in Woodsboro Park. Now she was going into another grave.

No, think of her in the clouds.

Joanne and Celia's mother, Jane, had agreed that the little gold cross be interred with Celia's remains. I felt it was a good decision.

A butterfly with brilliant colors flitted through the air and landed on a bouquet belonging to a neighboring grave. For a moment, it rested on a yellow lily, then flew away.

Think of Celia as a winged soul, freed from the dirt that had covered her body.

Mac Dalby stood on the fringe of the mourners, his eyes fixed on the new grave. He had told me in confidence that a solution was in sight. Then, in typical Mac Dalby fashion, he'd refused to say anything more except for this: "There's one last thread to tie. Those news stories brought people out of the woodwork. Suddenly, everybody's a witness."

"Are you going to make an arrest any time soon?" I asked.

"If I'm right, and I think I am, it's too late."

"Why? Is the killer dead?"

"Later," he said.

At the luncheon, I assumed. He'd promised to attend but couldn't stay long.

May her soul and the souls of all the faithful departed through the mercy of God rest in peace. Amen.

"Amen!" Brent's voice was too loud for this holy place. "Thank God, he's done praying. I'm hungry and hot."

"Shhh," I said, aware of a few turned heads and one muttered reproach.

As the mourners moved away from the grave, Annica murmured, "It's so sad, the way it ended."

I nodded and glanced at the shade trees again. "It's heartbreaking, but Celia has a pleasant resting place, and she's been in God's hands from the beginning."

Celia's mother, who resembled Joanne as she might look in eight or nine years, walked with a cane. Even with her sister's support, she moved unsteadily toward a white car. Joanne had issued an invitation for lunch at my house on Jonquil Lane, instructing those who were interested in one last gathering to follow her.

I let my thoughts travel on to Jonquil Lane and the spread Camille had offered to assemble. She had volunteered to bake mini-quiches and cakes. As hostess, I reviewed my grocery order, hoping there would be enough food for everyone. The crowd was twice as large as Joanne had anticipated. Obviously, she wanted to be the first to leave the cemetery, but Celia's mother walked slowly.

"I'm just glad it's over," Annica said.

But, of course, it wasn't. Not until Mac revealed what he had found out and what his intentions were. Unfortunately, Misty couldn't help him with that.

~ * ~

Camille had set the lunch out, buffet style, on the dining room table, and, miraculously managed to keep the dogs away from the food, although Candy wore a sly expression on her face, telling me she'd helped herself to one of the treats.

People, mostly strangers, filled the living room and spilled out to the porch where Camille and Gilbert had added their own patio furniture.

Away from the oppressive atmosphere that invariably hangs over a cemetery, I realized I was hungry. As I made myself a ham sandwich, Mac materialized at my side.

"I'll give you a hint," he said as he gulped his coffee. "I tracked down the man who drove the ice cream truck that day."

"Did he kill Celia?"

"I didn't say that. He has a good memory, and he provided a genuine clue which led me to—the answer."

The man was infuriating, dropping hints while backing away from the grand reveal.

"When are you going to share what you learned?" I asked.

"Soon. This food is great. It's too bad Crane is on duty."

Which was to be expected as it was early afternoon. I was about to ask who all Mac had interviewed when he said, "Duty calls." Setting his empty cup on the credenza, he strode away.

I followed him, stood on the porch, watching his cruiser enter Jonquil Lane. Maybe he'd confided in Crane. I'd have to be patient a little longer.

A crowd of admirers had gathered around Misty, showering her with praise and petting, along with handouts from the buffet. Knowing a good thing when she saw it, Candy had joined them.

"This is lovely," Joanne said. "I can't thank you enough."

"Camille did most of it."

I was happy to see she had found a free rocker and sat serenely with Jane, sipping tea and eating a muffin, her work done, the gathering a success.

"I wish I knew these people," I said.

"I don't know many of them myself, just the neighbors and several people who said they remember Celia. Some were at the park that day. The only one I recall is Marigold."

A shadow seemed to fall over her face. Marigold, Joanne's longtime friend. I didn't see her.

"Is she here?" I asked.

"She didn't come."

That was strange. Hardly the act of a friend.

"That policeman even interviewed me," Joanne said. "He implied I envied my sister because she had a child and I didn't."

Mac, I thought. *You went all out and kept on going.*

"So he's suggesting you killed Celia?"

"Yes. My dear goddaughter. My family."

"That's ridiculous, but I guess it's what makes Mac a good detective. The leave-no-stones-unturned approach."

Apparently, Mac hadn't told Joanne he'd as good as wrapped up the case. He certainly should have, but it wasn't my place to say anything.

"Hey, Camille! Any more of those little pies left?"

That could only be Brent.

I caught Camille's attention with a raised eyebrow and headed for the kitchen with Candy at my heels. Camille had stashed a dozen extra mini-quiches in the refrigerator. I could only hope they'd be enough to satisfy Brent's appetite.

Forty

That evening, Crane and I dined on leftovers. The quiches were gone, but instead of buying lunch meat, Camille had baked a whole ham, giving us enough food for another two meals or more. A bowl of potato salad and an orange sponge cake also remained.

While we ate, I told Crane about the burial and the mourners who had attended the luncheon at our house.

"About thirty people," I said. "Some of them claimed they were at Woodsboro Park that day, but no one saw Celia being taken."

He frowned. "I don't like the idea of strangers in the house when I'm not here. It's asking for trouble."

"From what Joanne said, I thought only a half dozen or so would show up. It was okay, though. Besides Mac, Brent and Gilbert were here all the time and, of course, all the dogs."

"Nevertheless..."

I passed him the cloverleaf rolls I'd baked to go with our dinner. "What exactly are you worried about?"

"First, you have a former student leaving weird notes in the mailbox."

"Yes, but..."

When I thought of Rusty, I imagined him working at a low-paying job in Oakpoint, perhaps delivering pizza. In his spare time, he would sneak over to Jonquil Lane to leave his cut-letter missives in our mailbox. I couldn't think of any way he could have known about Celia's remains being found or the funeral.

Unless he read the *Banner*, which was unlikely. Even then, he wouldn't know about the luncheon, which was a last-minute affair.

"Everyone I saw looked over thirty," I said, which seemed to satisfy Crane. "Mac claims he knows who killed Celia. Did he tell you?"

"I haven't seen him. If he's figured it out, what's he waiting for?"

"A thread to tie. But maybe he'll tell you and you can tell me."

He smiled. "Maybe. This is the first cold case Dalby has solved, and he's been playing around with them for years."

"It wouldn't have happened without Misty."

"Remind him of that," Crane said.

It wasn't until much later that I recalled Crane hadn't mentioned his second reason for worrying.

~ * ~

The near-drought ended with a shower that lasted long enough to revive the earth. Under a pure blue sky, the leaves and flowers shimmered with new life. In the fresh, sweet air, the collies regained their lost energy. It was as if spring were beginning all over again.

I took the dogs outside to play and sat on the porch drinking lemonade and contemplating the shiny new Frisbee at my feet. As soon as I finished my drink, I would join them.

June was winding down, my vacation was slipping away, and Rainbow and Ellalyn were still missing. Yesterday, I had driven by Ellalyn's house on my way home from Blackbourne's Grocers. It still had an unmistakable look of utter abandonment, even though the grass had been mowed, and no mail spilled out of the mailbox onto the porch.

However, the drapes remained closed against all comers. I knocked on the door but this time didn't hear a sound from within. If only I could solve my own mystery. Perhaps I should ask Mac, super detective, for help.

On the way home, I considered reminding him about the ongoing case but rejected the idea. He still hadn't revealed the identity of Celia's killer—if indeed he knew it—not to Crane, not even to Joanne, as I learned in a brief phone call I'd made to find out how she was doing.

"I don't think we'll ever know who killed Celia," Joanne had said, "but somehow I'm at peace now that I know where she is."

"I'm glad."

"Thanks to your wonderful collie. Only I'm puzzled. My friend, Marigold, has dropped out of sight. This morning, a 'For Sale' sign went up at her house. She doesn't answer her cell. I hope we don't have another disappearance to deal with."

Marigold. She who had befriended Joanne after Celia vanished and remained her close friend for two decades.

Was it possible Marigold Asher had killed Celia? If so, that would have been a long deception.

But what possible motive could Marigold have had? I reminded myself that I didn't know anything about her. She appeared to be devoted to Joanne, if not particularly supportive.

I recalled what Mac had said about the driver of the ice cream truck, the man with the good memory. If he'd given Mac an essential cue, he couldn't be the killer.

Who then?

A random stranger?

We weren't exactly drowning in suspects.

When I thought about Celia's killer, the image of a sinister looking man formed in my mind. He had a sly, secretive look, straggly dark hair, and hid his beady eyes behind sunglasses. He stopped short of having a black cape to twirl. A typical textbook villain then.

My mind wandered down first one unconsidered trail, then another.

Had Celia known Marigold? Probably not, as Celia hadn't lived on Joanne's street and Joanne had only met Marigold after Celia vanished.

Suddenly, I had had enough idle speculation. I'd soon know the answer to the puzzle, unless Mac decided to make us wait a little longer for the big reveal.

Candy had sidled up to the porch with a yip and gave the Frisbee a shove in my direction.

Play with me!

I rose and tossed it across the flower beds onto the grass, thankful that amid thoughts of death, I was alive to play with my dogs.

Forty-one

The fresh spring-like days ended as abruptly as the drought. As I enjoyed a second breakfast of tea and cinnamon rolls on the porch the next day, the muggy air seemed to tighten itself around me. I took a deep breath, simply to make sure I still could.

The collies roamed listlessly through the front yard, toys forgotten, and returned frequently to lap water from their large communal water bowl.

The weather forecast contained a mishmash of summertime cliches: hazy, humid, storms. It was too hot to do anything more strenuous than retire to the air-conditioned living room with my latest library Gothic.

The pack came to life as a collie running free appeared on Jonquil Lane. It proved to be no interloper, but a friend, Ginger. Moments later, Jennifer and Molly came into view, running themselves and waving madly with the energy and exuberance of the young.

Ginger leaped to the top of the stairs, her eyes on the Frisbee, while Molly flopped down on the top step. The collies milled around, tails wagging, eyes bright with anticipated fun.

"Hey, Jennet!" Jennifer said. "Good! You're home. We have something to tell you."

"Something good," Molly added.

"Yeah, Rainbow's back."

"What? Where?" I left the last bite of cinnamon roll unattended and Candy grabbed it.

"She's at the park," Jennifer said. "Woodsboro Park. We saw her."

"From a distance," Molly said. "But it was Rainbow. She had that streak of black fur on her collar."

"Slow down. Now, from the beginning."

Jennifer leaned back on the porch post and pushed her long hair out of her face. "Our neighbor Jess and a bunch of us were at the park when we saw a tricolor collie come out of the woods. Molly called her and she ran off."

"So we chased her," Molly said. "But she got away."

"Was Ginger with you?" I asked.

"No, we left her home. We just picked her up and came right over to tell you. Jess went on back to the park."

"You'll go with us, won't you?" Jennifer said.

Return to Woodsboro Park? After Misty had uncovered Celia's skeleton, I never planned to set foot in that park again. Some time ago, Miss Eidt had called it evil or unlucky. I couldn't remember her exact words. I did know it had the most unpleasant of associations for me. Acreage carved out of the wilderness to provide a sylvan paradise for the denizens of Foxglove Corners who didn't have enough woods and waters around their homes to satisfy them.

A place where Evil felt at home.

But this was the first time anyone had seen Rainbow since the Collie Walkabout.

Once I'd wondered whether Rainbow had ever left the park. What if she'd been there along? Hiding? Or being hidden from sight?

After all our searches, that was extremely unlikely. She could, however, have returned to the last place she had been with Ellalyn, looking for her.

"Jennet?"

Jennifer was waiting for an answer.

"I'm thinking," I said.

About hours of free time until Crane came home. About *Haldane Station*, which I was re-reading and thoroughly enjoying. About the haze and humidity and predicted storms.

About Rainbow.

"We're not the only ones who saw her," Molly said. "We asked around. Jess was with us, and a lady saw a black collie eating a sandwich some kid threw away."

I wanted to believe the dog was Rainbow, but the urge to play devil's advocate took over. "There's more than one tricolor in the area. I have three tris myself."

"Yeah," Molly said, "but most of them have full white collars. This one had black breaking through the white."

"Even that isn't unusual."

"Don't you want to find her?" Jennifer demanded.

I wanted nothing more. They must know that. Assuming we saw the black collie, would she come to me? She didn't know me. For all that I'd devoted hours to searching for Ellalyn's missing collie, I'd never set eyes on her. If by chance I saw her, I knew enough not to chase a dog.

I glanced down at my blue sundress. It was new, never intended for tramping through woods.

"What are we waiting for?" I asked. "Just give me a few minutes to change."

~ * ~

After a quick call to Camille to ask her to look out for the dogs while I was away, I changed into jeans and a white top with long sleeves to guard against sunburn and mosquito bites. I never knew where I'd end up.

Before leaving, I filled a bag with dog treats. If Rainbow were reduced to scrounging for discarded sandwiches, surely she could be enticed with liver tartlets from Pluto's Gourmet Pet Shop.

We dropped Ginger off at Molly's house. I'd considered taking Misty with us but decided against it, mainly because of the heat. She would be happiest sleeping in a cool house with her sisters, and I wouldn't have need of her special talents today.

So we set out, our hopes for finding Rainbow high.

Strangely the park seemed deserted, although it couldn't be. I reminded myself how large it was. The thick woods muted sounds of conversation and laughter, creating an eerie feeling that all of the park goers were living their lives in another dimension.

Where should we begin?

"Our friends staked out a place at the lake," Jennifer said. "We were at the gazebo taking pictures when we saw Rainbow."

"Let's start there then."

We entered the path Brent and I had traversed on the day of Rainbow's disappearance, calling Rainbow's name at intervals and occasionally slapping away mosquitoes.

The woods are silent, dark, and deep, I thought. *They have a life of their own. Monstrous beings live here. They inhabit the limbs of trees. They reach out for intruders...*

I thought I'd dread revisiting the place where Misty had dug her fateful hole, but surprisingly, the area had lost the grim ambience of that day. The holes had been filled, the grave covered with new grass, and climbing red roses wrapped around the graceful gazebo.

In years to come, no one would remember that the skeleton of a murdered child had been unearthed nearby. Just as most people had forgotten about the boy who had drowned in the fountain.

"I'm going inside," Molly announced.

Jennifer followed her, but both girls came to a sudden top at the entrance. Molly grabbed a branch to steady herself and cried out as a thorn stabbed her finger.

"Jennet you have to see this," Jennifer said.

Ignoring the chill that shuddered through my body, I hurried to the gazebo.

Please. Not something horrible.

Forty-two

In a sense it was something horrible, although not the body I'd been half expecting.

A long pink cardigan lay in a corner of the gazebo. It had a classic shawl collar and a torn sleeve—and a stain across the front that looked like fresh blood. A trail of bright red drops, mixed with the rose petals that had blown inside, led straight to the sweater. Whoever had worn the garment must be wounded. But where was she?

"It looks like cashmere." Molly advanced toward the garment as Jennifer said sharply, "Don't touch it!"

"We'd better report it to the ranger," I said, picturing a person wandering through the park, dripping blood in her wake or perhaps lying still beneath the trees, having succumbed to her injury.

Woodsboro Park Claims Another Victim.

And what of the person responsible for the attack? Another killer hiding in the woods? Or even closer?

"Whatever happened here..." In spite of her tan, Molly's face had lost its color. "We were only a few minutes away. Just down at the lake."

"Could the sweater have belonged to one of your friends?" I asked.

"No way," Jennifer said. "None of us would wear anything like this."

Molly added, "Besides, it's too hot. It must be ninety."

"At least." I felt every bit of the heat and humidity. With the thought of humidity, I pulled a cloth napkin out of my bag of treats and ran it over my neck, which still felt damp.

Did the wearer remove the sweater because she was too hot? Or because of the unsightly blood stain? Probably because of the blood. What did she do then? She might have left an additional trail of blood on the grass. I hadn't noticed anything leading up to the gazebo except for fresh green turf.

Molly was trembling. I laid my hand on her shoulder.

"This place is dangerous," I said. "Let's find the ranger and remember why we came to the park."

"Rainbow," Jennifer murmured. "I hope she's okay."

Ellalyn, I thought.

One time, when I'd seen her at the Green House, she was wearing pink, an old-fashioned blouse with lace and ruffles meant to advertise the shop's vintage clothing. She had once confided that pink was her favorite color.

Please don't let it be her.

~ * ~

After we found Ranger Rob Leighton and turned the matter of the bloody sweater over to him, Jennifer said, "Let's go back to the lake. Maybe one of the kids heard something."

"Like a scream," Molly said.

I didn't object. The girls had seen Rainbow in that section of the park. Of course, she could be anywhere by then. Now that I thought about it, I might have gone on a fool's errand today and only added another mystery to the mix.

Or did the stained sweater connect to the main mystery? It was difficult to know, but Woodsboro Park was certainly living up to its reputation. With the best of intentions, we had wandered into danger.

"Maybe one of your friends saw Rainbow again," I said.

The lake had an entrancing blue shimmer in the sunlight. I had a sudden longing to wade into the water, to feel its cool touch on my body. To be wearing a bathing suit instead of jeans and a top.

"We're over there, under the tree." Molly pointed to a dozen or so young people lounging on blankets, drinking pop, and listening to music, oblivious of foul deeds.

Molly and Jennifer raced ahead of me. I heard Molly say, "Did you guys see the black collie again?" as my attention came to rest on a familiar face topped by a mop of disheveled red hair.

It couldn't be...he was in Oakpoint delivering pizzas. Or on Jonquil Lane slipping a threatening message into my mailbox.

"Hey guys! It's Mrs. Ferguson," Rusty said.

"Do you know Jennet? Molly asked.

"She's my English teacher," he said, with a grin that appeared to be friendly.

All past grievances forgotten? I didn't think so. I also didn't think he would allude to our past history as it would involve admitting he hadn't graduated with his class.

"What are you doing here?" I asked.

His eyes retained a trace of an arrogant gleam. "Just chillin'. Same as you."

"Rusty and Jess are going together," Jennifer said.

I was momentarily surprised, but why should I be? I tended to think of Molly and Jennifer as little girls peddling lemonade and cookies at a makeshift stand, but they were in high school, old enough to have boyfriends. Rusty was their contemporary, and I had to admit he was an attractive young man when he wasn't sneering or whining or campaigning for an illegal credit.

"I'm going to see if the ranger found out anything, and I'll keep an eye out for Rainbow," I said.

Jess opened a can of pop. "We'll get Molly and Jen home."

I left them there, enjoying the sunshine and water, and re-entered the trail that would eventually bring me to the ranger's hut at the park's entrance and the parking lot.

I felt shaken by the sight of Rusty among the girls' friends. He hadn't made a single threatening move or uttered a word that could contain a double meaning. It was as if Oakpoint graduation day having come and gone, it was also forgotten, soaked up in the summertime sun. As if a teacher met out of context became an instant friend.

Nonetheless, the memory of those threats burned in my mind. I couldn't get away from the group at the lake fast enough.

~ * ~

Dark woods hemmed me in on both sides. I had left the sun behind and might as well have left civilization as well, for the heavy silence that pressed on me.

As I passed the gazebo, I glanced inside. The sweater was still there, crumpled in the corner. Had the ranger visited the scene yet or even called the police? Perhaps I hadn't impressed on him the urgency of the situation.

If the sweater's owner were hoping for help, she would be disappointed. She might even die waiting.

As for myself, I had checked out the park as intended. Now the time had come to resume my planned day, to read *Haldane Station* in air-cooled comfort. If Rainbow roamed the park, most likely she would be here another day. I'd call Brent, who would be happy to join me in a new search now that we had a genuine sighting.

Sounds shattered the silence. A definite rustle in the woods followed by a loud crack as if a heavy foot had trod down hard on a branch.

An animal? Rainbow?

Not seeing anything, I walked a little faster. Every nerve in my body slid into high alert.

Run! Run for your life!

A bolt of pain exploded between my shoulder blades, propelling me forward into the hard-packed dirt of the trail.

Gunshot? Rock? A blow from an invisible fist?

The pain spread throughout my body. It stole my breath and ability to move.

But I *had* to move. I tried to get up, to force myself to stand, but the pain pushed me back down to the ground. The colors of the woods, myriad shades of green, turned to gray, then to black, then to nothing.

Forty-three

Time slipped into reverse. I was back on the trail, heading for the park ranger's hut in a green vehicle made of wood and leaves, but I wasn't driving. Then who was? The trail seemed twice as long as it had when I'd traversed it with Molly and Jennifer looking for...

I simply couldn't remember. Someone who had disappeared. Celia?

The trail went on and on. Then after the fashion of all dreams, I was flung to the forest floor. My back felt as if an axe had cut into it. Maybe that was what had happened. I tried to think, but my head was pounding, and I couldn't cry out. My voice didn't work.

Nothing was as it should be or would ever be again. I might as well surrender to the inevitable and stay asleep or unconscious. Or dead.

~ * ~

"Are you all right? Janet?"

I opened my eyes. I recognized the voice. "Jennet," I said. "It's Jennet." A lamp shone in my face, intensifying the pounding. My eyes closed again.

"Sorry. Jennet. How do you feel?"

"Terrible," I said. "Everything hurts."

I tried to lift my arm to reach my shoulders, and a sharp pain sliced through it.

"But I don't think anything's broken," I said. "Someone threw something at me, and I fell and lost consciousness."

"I was beginning to think you'd never wake up. Did you see who did it?"

"No, I thought I was alone. He must have come out of the woods."

"Something similar happened to me."

Find out who's talking, I told myself. *What place is this? How did I get here?*

"My name is Ellalyn," my companion said. "You remember me, don't you?"

She was dressed as I was, only in beige pants, and her sleeveless ivory top bore an unsightly reddish stain.

"Of course I do. Does the pink cardigan in the gazebo belong to you?"

"It does. I left it behind after I ran into a branch as sharp as a knife." Frowning, she touched the stain on her tank top. "It was my favorite sweater, but that's the least of my problems."

I reached in my pocket for my cell phone. Nothing was there except the clammy napkin from the bag of treats. And where were they?

"You just vanished," I said. "I've been looking for you."

She attempted a smile. "Well, you found me."

"Where are we?"

"In somebody's basement. I don't know where."

All I could see were gray walls and pillars supporting an unfinished ceiling—and three narrow cobweb-encrusted windows. Like most basements, it contained a furnace, a hot water tank, a washing machine and a dryer, together with a jumble of unwanted furniture in no particular order. The shade belonging to the lamp that shone so bravely in the dimness was in tatters.

"We're in the country somewhere," Ellalyn said. "I stood on a table and looked through the window. There aren't any other houses around."

"Could we get out that way?"

"I thought about it, but the locks are frozen, and I couldn't find anything to break the glass."

There were two of us now. Perhaps the window was a possibility. I'd conduct my own search in a while. Now I had a more immediate concern.

"Is there any water besides from the tap?" I asked.

"Some."

She opened a bottle of Michigan Pure and handed it to me. I took a tentative sip and quickly drained it.

"That's so good," I said. "I've never been so thirsty."

Ellalyn reached for another bottle. "We have food, too, such as it is. A loaf of white bread several days old, I'd guess, and a jar of peanut butter. Some bananas. They're too ripe, but beggars can't be choosers. I guess we can live on that for a while."

"Have you been here long?" I asked.

"Since this morning. It feels longer."

Camille would be getting concerned about me by now. And Crane? He'd be home. Or would he? I wasn't wearing my watch.

"Is there a serial kidnapper running around in the park?" I asked.

She gave a wry smile. "There might as well be."

"Do you know who did this?"

"I think so, but I didn't see him," she said.

"I didn't see my attacker either."

I wanted to go back to sleep and wake up in our house on Jonquil Lane with a bottle of headache pills in the bathroom cabinet. None of this had happened, and...

What precisely was this? What had happened?

I had no idea. My eyes began to close.

"No!" Ellalyn said. "Jennet. You have to stay awake."

I didn't have to do anything—but die.

~ * ~

The next time I woke up, things were clearer.

What things?

My situation, for one. I had been attacked and taken from Woodsboro Park. I'd left Jennifer and Molly and their friends and somehow lost my cell phone. No one knew where I was.

But I'd told the girls I was on my way to the ranger's hut, and my car was parked in the lot.

That was good then.

But I still didn't know where I was. Where *we* were, that is. I had found Ellalyn and managed to lose myself.

Woodsboro Park strikes again.

Ellalyn had made herself a sandwich, which she ate sitting on a battered kitchen table, circa 1955, with no apparent relish. Well, peanut butter was a far cry from bacon, lettuce, and tomato.

"Do you feel better now?" she asked.

"Moderately."

"Are you hungry?"

"A little."

I should be. I had a vague memory of eating cinnamon rolls. How long ago was that? And hadn't Candy grabbed what she considered her fair share of my snack?

"What I really want is to know where I am and how I got here and who attacked me and why and…"

She cut into my rambling. "Let's begin at the beginning."

"Good. There's so much I don't know. Is it true that you went on vacation with your boyfriend?"

"That's what I wanted people to think," she said. "I have a cabin up north. It's off the beaten path, and nobody knows about it. I needed to get away," she added. "It was life or death."

"Without your dog?"

"I didn't know where Rainbow was, and I couldn't stay." Her voice trembled, begged me to understand. "You and your friend promised to look for her."

"We did, and Brent Fowler offered a reward for her return, but we never found her or heard anything about her until today. You remember Jennifer and Molly? They saw a tricolor collie in Woodsboro Park and tried to catch her."

"I heard that rumor, too, but I didn't see her."

Facts swirled around me. Ellalyn was omitting whole segments of her story.

"Would you mind backtracking for a moment?" I asked. "Why did you need to get away?"

She sighed. "I guess I can talk about it now. I overheard some information by accident and felt I had to pass it on. But in doing so, I crossed the wrong person. Rainbow was taken from me as a punishment. The best way to hurt a woman is through the dog she loves, and I was pretty sure that was only the beginning."

"When we spoke some time ago, you said you didn't have any enemies," I reminded her.

"I remember. Belatedly, it occurred to me that I'd already talked too much."

If Ellalyn were one of my students, I would have asked her to be specific, to use concrete details. But as she hesitated and talked around things she dared not say, all of the puzzle pieces that had been flying around without direction came together in my mind.

"You were running away from the Michigan Militia, weren't you? That plot to abduct Representative Justina Granville. You were the anonymous informant."

"I was, to my everlasting regret," she said.

Forty-four

We sat on an old rose sofa that had suffered several tears and was losing its stuffing. The lamp with the tattered shade cast a feeble glow on us and brought the shadows out of hiding. The atmosphere was conducive to confidences.

"When you disappeared, you were running away from Garth MacKay, then," I said.

"Not Garth. His partner, Greg Sky."

"Was Greg really your boyfriend?"

"For about two weeks, then we broke up with a bang. I don't need proof to know he was responsible for taking Rainbow and leaving that other dog in her place. When he was arrested, I thought it was safe to come home. Guess I was wrong."

"I'm pretty sure he's still in custody," I said.

"Then who...?" She trailed off. "Who did this?"

"One of his militia friends?"

"It's possible, but they'd just met me."

"Still, they may know what you did."

She nodded slowly in silent agreement. "That's right. They're a close-knit group. I was the outsider, and I sensed they didn't approve of me for Greg. I don't know how they found out, though. My information was supposed to be confidential."

"I don't understand why I was attacked," I said. "All I knew was what I read in the paper. I'm not the slightest bit knowledgeable about militia activities. This sounds a lot like the plan to kidnap Justina."

Ellalyn said, "It may be something else."

"Maybe."

I hadn't mentioned Rusty to Ellalyn, but that didn't mean I wasn't wondering if he were my assailant. Perhaps the friendly grin was all for show and he still wanted his revenge. He would have seen me enter the trail, made an excuse to leave the group, and follow me, setting his plan in motion.

Was I sorry now? Oh, yes. No doubt about it.

Whether I was paying for my own decision to prevent Rusty from graduating, or somehow sharing Ellalyn's whistleblower status, I could clearly picture the elephant in the room. Its name was Our Fate, and it was pacing from one end of the basement to the other, waiting to be noticed.

Finally, I said, "Surely, they aren't going to kill us."

She shuddered. "Let's hope not."

"It would have been easier to do that in the park," I pointed out.

"Not really," Ellalyn said. "There's always the chance that someone would pop out of the woods. This basement in no man's land is totally private."

I rose, trying to hold in assorted groans and wishing fervently for a pain pill.

"We can't just wait here like sitting ducks," I said. "Let's try to break down the door again."

We had already made several attempts, but the door at the top of the narrow staircase hadn't budged, not an inch. There wasn't room for a proper assault on it. Neither of us wanted to complicate our situation by falling down the stairs.

Nor was there any implement we could use to break the windows. It appeared the owner had stripped the house and basement bare of tools, of anything that could be moved easily to a new location. Possibly he planned to leave the discarded furniture here.

Ellalyn gazed with loathing at the sustenance our jailer had provided for us. "I wish I'd never said anything to the police. I could have pretended not to hear them talking and just walked away."

She had uttered several previous variants of this sentiment throughout the day. I reminded her that nobody could undo the past, but we might be able to alter our possible future. It remained to be seen how we could do that.

"Did you know Greg was a member of the militia when you were dating him?" I asked.

"I didn't even know it existed. Greg was so sweet and unassuming. He liked horses. He wanted buy a farm and breed them. He just seemed so wholesome, like a cowboy."

"Or a Hollywood version of one."

"I was deceived. I let myself be deceived.

However interesting, this trip down memory lane wasn't helping us. I said, "We *have* to get out of here."

"There's no way," Ellalyn said. "Nobody knows I came back. I was going to call Zara but put it off." She added, "My car is in the Woodsboro lot."

"So is mine. Won't they check on vehicles left there through the night?"

"They should."

What good would that do, though? The car, even if it could talk, didn't know what had happened to me.

The elephant having been acknowledged faded along with the light. I wished I'd thought to wear my watch. It must be around six or seven.

By then, Crane would know I was unable to come home. He would drive out to Woodsboro Park to find my car abandoned. He'd call Jennifer and Molly, but all they could tell him was that I had left the park.

Left the park but never made it to the lot.

He knew I would never leave the collies alone all day, even with the knowledge that Camille was watching them. And I always, always had his dinner ready when he came home.

What would he do? What *could* he do?

If I'd taken Misty with me, would the events have unraveled in a different direction? Or would my kidnapper have killed her?

I sent a silent message to Misty. *I'm here, and I need help. I don't know where 'here' is, but I know you can find me, Misty. Hurry!*

I created a comforting video in my mind and kept the scenario playing: Misty on the hunt for her owner, Crane close behind. Rescue right around the corner. It could happen. Couldn't it?

Misty was no Lassie, but she was all I had.

~ * ~

As night fell, I grew despondent. I'd given Misty an impossible task. Ellalyn had fallen asleep, and I had been so hungry I'd smeared a dab of peanut butter on bread with my finger and tried not to think that the bread was stale. The bottled water was lukewarm. Was this to be my last meal?

In the past, I had taken chances, courted disaster without looking ahead. Today, I'd simply gone to Woodsboro Park—where Celia Loring had disappeared, and a little boy had drowned in a park—to continue my search for somebody else's dog.

Where was the fairness in that?

My life had been so happy. I'd been given everything I ever dreamed of. The perfect husband, many collies where once I'd had one, a green Victorian farmhouse in Foxglove Corners. Home. I had foolishly believed it would go on forever.

Nothing ever does.

Another bite of dry peanut butter on stale bread would choke me.

I couldn't stop the tears.

I was going to lose it all.

I'd already lost, because there was no way Misty could find me.

It was over.

Forty-five

During the night, the storm arrived with high winds that grew progressively stronger. It seemed to last forever. Thunder crashed directly overhead and heavy rain lashed the narrow windows. Lightning flashes threw the basement into brief clarity. I prayed for safety from the elements, then simply for safety.

At some point, the storm moved on, and the night grew quiet except for a hypnotic dripping sound. In the sudden silence, I thought I heard Crane's voice calling my name. I could almost see his face, the silver streaks in his blond hair, and his gray eyes with their frosty flecks; and I almost answered him.

Alas, it was an illusion. Wishful thinking.

Finally, I fell into an uneasy sleep and woke to an awareness of pain in new places, weak light streaming through the basement windows, and a strong sense of something off. Then, I heard footsteps on the floor above. The walker made no attempt to move quietly through the house. That was ominous.

"Do you hear that?" Ellalyn whispered. "This is it, Jennet. What can we do?"

I swallowed away the dryness in my mouth that made me feel as if I were gagged.

"Be ready for anything," I said.

If these were to be my last minutes on earth, they had to count. I tried to pray, but my mind couldn't find the words. We had one slight advantage. Only one person was walking through the house, and there were two of us.

I stood, frozen in place, and waited.

The door squeaked open, and a young red-haired man stood at the top of the stairs glaring down at us. Rusty! I knew it. He didn't have a weapon, none that I could see, that is.

"Are you two okay down there?" he asked.

"We're alive, no thanks to you," Ellalyn snapped.

"You're in real trouble now, Rusty," I said. "Kidnapping is a federal offense. Why did you do it?"

"We got no time for questions, Mrs. Ferguson. Hurry up. You guys are getting out of here."

That was it? I let my indignation and my questions go and climbed the staircase, reaching in vain for a railing that didn't exist. Ellelyn stumbled along behind me.

When we were on the other side of the door, Rusty locked it and led us through the quiet house. I had seen this living room before through the front window. The grand piano was gone, as was all of the furniture, along with every homey decorative touch.

We were in the farmhouse on North Windmill Road, the militia hangout. It was now an empty shell, full of morning shadows and unspoken threats.

How did Rusty know about this place? Certainly, the Michigan Militia didn't recruit their members fresh out of high school. I didn't want to follow that train of thought.

He seemed different, though, aged in a matter of weeks. The whiny, self-centered teenager was suddenly serious and resolute. And it suddenly struck me that he resembled someone I'd seen recently. I couldn't make the connection, but I was sure I was right.

"Is this about your graduation credit, Rusty?" I asked. "Because if it is, Ellalyn had nothing to do with it."

Instead of answering, he said, "You don't have to know anything. I'm taking you two back to the park. You can get yourselves home from there. Forget about all this. It never happened."

"But it did," Ellalyn said, "and you'll pay for it. I have a friend who's a police officer."

Ignoring her, he opened the front door to a gust of muggy air. The storm had ushered in another heat wave, but after being confined in the basement of the closed-up house, even the heat was a blessing. I felt as if I were taking my first breath.

The white Honda parked in front of the house was running, its passenger side door half-open. There was no traffic on Windmill Road, no one to help us. But if Rusty had spoken the truth, if he was taking us back to Woodsboro Park, maybe this was a true deliverance, which left me with one major question.

What was the point of this strange abduction and even stranger rescue?

"Get in," he said.

Ordinarily, I would never enter an unknown vehicle, but in this instance, we didn't have a choice.

~ * ~

A seemingly endless road stretched out in front of us. Glowering woods lining either side cast us into a perpetual dimness.

Were we really going to Woodsboro Park?

Rusty refused to answer questions. He didn't speak. He drove too fast for the curving roads and seemed distracted. From time to time, he glanced in the rear-view mirror as if he thought we were being followed, even though curves hid a possible pursuing car from view.

I didn't recognize the roads he took and wondered if he were heading to some distance place where our bodies would never be found, and no one would connect our deaths to the Michigan Militia.

Therefore, when we reached the park, I was relieved, but at the same time apprehensive. The entrance was already crowded. The crush conveyed a welcome sense of security to the scene. Nothing too terrible could happen in the midst of so many witnesses. Or could it?

I spied my car baking in the early morning sun, but otherwise all right.

"Now, you get out," Rusty said. "Don't say a word to anyone about this. Make up some excuse for staying out all night."

"Right," I said.

What planet did Rusty inhabit? I was certain Crane had reported that I was missing and was doing everything in his power to find me.

He pulled a cell phone out of his pocket and tossed it to me. *My* cell phone. I caught it before it fell to the ground.

"Don't go calling the police if you know what's good for you," he said.

I exited the car without speaking and stood with Ellalyn watching Rusty drive away. Thank heavens. I held my phone to the light and, of course, the battery needed charging. A setback of minutes as I was sure Ranger Leighton would let me borrow his phone.

"Where do you know that kid from?" Ellalyn asked.

"He was my student," I said, adding, "I'm an English teacher. We had a difference of opinion, and he didn't graduate."

"Some difference of opinion," she said.

I wasn't sure what to think but decided not to accuse Rusty of abducting me. Not yet.

"After yesterday, I'm afraid to go home and afraid to stay in the park," Ellalyn said. "Rainbow is still here somewhere. I don't know what to do."

"Do you really have a policeman friend?" I asked.

"No. I hoped that would rattle him, but he didn't react."

"Well, I do, and my husband is a deputy sheriff. Why don't you come home with me? We'll figure everything out."

"I can't leave my car in the park any longer," she said. "I'm just glad it's still here."

"Drive it, then. Follow me home. And let's get on the road before another kidnapper shows up."

Forty-six

Finally, things were going my way. Ranger Leighton lent me his cell phone, was satisfied with our minimal explanation, and gave us a chocolate bar, which we split.

"I still have that sweater," he said. "Nobody ever claimed it."

"She'll turn up eventually." But I wondered if Ellalyn would want it back. She stood at my side, listening but not reacting.

I called Crane and assured him several times that I was unharmed, leaving out the part about the rock—or whatever it was—thrown at me.

"I didn't see who snatched me," I said. "As soon as I'm home, I'll tell you the whole story, and we'll take it from there."

"Stay where you are. Brent and I will come get you, and Brent will drive your car home," he said in that familiar dictatorial deputy sheriff voice he brought out on occasion.

I didn't want to wait in Woodsboro Park another minute lest my newfound freedom would be wrested from me in yet another way.

"I'll be home sooner if I drive myself," I said. "I really am all right, just a little hungry. Actually, I'm starved. I'm bringing Ellalyn Zoller with me."

"You found Ellalyn? What does she have to do with this?" he demanded.

"She was kidnapped, too. We were together."

It was unlike Crane to capitulate and unlike me to deny his request. But—

"I'd better get started," I said. "I can't wait to get home."

"If you're sure..."

On the way home, I kept thinking about Rusty's role in my misadventure. I found it hard to believe he had kidnapped me as part of a demented revenge plot. No matter how angry he was, I couldn't imagine him attacking me. I couldn't remember a single instance of physical violence directed toward a Marston teacher by a student.

Also, if he were working alone, how could he concoct such an outrageous scheme? And, most important, why had he freed me?

The militia connection made a grim kind of sense. Rusty had access to the farmhouse. Being part of a splinter group would appeal to his rebellious streak. Ellalyn had betrayed Greg Sky, inviting retaliation from his friends. How I'd been dragged into her affairs remained a mystery.

Then there was the fact that Rusty resembled someone whose name I couldn't recall. He was young. Older than Rusty. His hair wasn't red. He was...

At that point, the memories deserted me.

Every mile brought me closer to Jonquil Lane and, I sincerely hoped, to answers, and perhaps to payback of my own.

~ * ~

Vehicles spilled out of our driveway onto the grass, one of them being Mac's patrol car. Every light in the house appeared to be on, and the happy sounds of eight collies barking greeted me. I was home sweet home.

Crane was waiting for me in the doorway. He closed the distance between us with long strides and caught me up in his arms. Halley and Misty had sneaked out with him and danced joyfully around us. Brent materialized on the porch, a coffee mug in his hand, with Camille at his side.

It was mid-morning, the sun was bright, and my life was beginning again after being rudely interrupted. For the first time since my capture, I was aware of the sad state of my jeans and my crumpled white top. My wish for a shower and a fresh dress almost took precedence over food.

Ellalyn parked her car and stood uncertainly behind me. She didn't know Crane and most likely didn't remember Brent from the Collie Walkabout.

"I was afraid I'd never see you again." Crane buried his face in my hair. "I wondered if you'd found another Huron Court and got zapped back into another time."

"There was nothing supernatural about what happened to me," I said, reaching out to touch Ellalyn's arm. "This is Ellalyn Zoller, Rainbow's owner. Ellalyn, my husband, Crane."

"The wanderer returns!" Brent boomed out from the porch.

"Why is everyone here?" I asked. "Did you wait for me to disappear to have a party?"

"Something like that," Brent said. "Come in and tell us all about it. And you don't have to call the police. They're here."

~ * ~

We sat around the oak table in the kitchen—Crane and Ellalyn and the friends I feared I'd never see again. Annica had stopped by on her way to Clovers, and Camille was frying bacon and eggs for all of us. I had postponed my bath in favor of breakfast.

"Were you looking for me, Mac?" I asked.

"I was, but when I heard you were on your way home, I dropped by to give you the name of Celia Loring's killer. I thought that'd cheer you up."

"Who was it?"

"That can wait," Crane said. "First, I want to hear Jennet's story."

I wanted to tell it. Perhaps they'd pick up on something I missed.

"You know I went to the park because Molly and Jennifer saw Rainbow there?"

He nodded.

"We didn't find Rainbow, but I saw Rusty Delmar at the lake with a group of the girls' friends. I was just walking along the trail at the park, heading home, when something hard hit me in the back. I fell and lost consciousness. Ellalyn had a similar experience."

I related the entire harrowing tale, including the vile food that had been set out for us.

"This morning, Rusty showed up and made us go back to the park. I realized we were in the militia hangout."

"That student of yours?" Crane asked.

"Rusty, yes.

He drank his coffee quietly. I knew he was trying to make sense of the story. I wished him luck as I was still floundering.

"That's carrying payback too far," he said.

"I don't think Rusty was the one who attacked me."

"Then who?"

"I wish I knew."

"When we find the guilty party, you're going to press charges," Mac said.

"I want to. Make Rusty talk. He must know who else was involved."

"Let me give you some names," Ellalyn said. "Claud and Chet Lanier. They're related. Joe Farley and Allan Dale. They're all Greg Sky's friends."

As Mac jotted down Ellalyn's information in his notebook, Brent said, "We looked all over hell for you, Jennet, even when it started raining. We drove by the farmhouse, but it was dark."

"We were locked in the basement," I said. "We had a lamp on."

"We didn't see any light. Then we stopped at that house with the canoe. You remember that guy who had his hands all over the Plymouth?"

I did, and on the heels of the memory came a flash of enlightenment.

The other man, Claud. Dye his hair red, take away ten years, and you had Rusty Delmar. They might be brothers or cousins. Was Rusty with them when he wasn't in my class? With the Michigan Militia?

"They sure knew a lot about that farmhouse," Brent said.

I knew we were finally on the right track. "Go get them, Mac."

Camille set plates of bacon on the table and began serving eggs.

Crane rose. "I'm not hungry."

"Well, I am." I felt I could eat my breakfast and Crane's, too.

Crane dropped a kiss on my head and said, "We'll be back with that kid's head on a platter."

I shuddered at the grisly image. I didn't want that for Rusty, no matter what he might have done. He had been my student, after all. He was young, with his whole life ahead of him."

Ellalyn said, "I want whoever did this to pay the price, but I'm afraid of what they'll do next. Look what happened the last time I interfered."

"You followed your conscience," I said.

As Crane and Mac went through the door, I realized Mac hadn't told us who had killed Celia. Oh well, a cold case would keep. Apprehending the kidnappers wouldn't.

Forty-seven

Brent, ever the gallant, offered to accompany Ellalyn to her house, promising to check every room for an intruder. Annica left for her shift at Clovers, Camille went home, and I found myself alone with my beautiful collies.

Every little thing I did was touched with joy. Pouring lilac-scented bubble bath into the tub, donning a crisp clean dress and playing ball with the dogs. Getting dirty again.

Everything in life becomes more precious when you think you're about to lose it.

Now if Mac could find the kidnappers and put them behind bars, I could rest more easily. At the moment, I wondered if they still lurked in the shadows waiting to take back their captives.

I had my dogs to protect me, but Ellalyn didn't have Rainbow.

Inevitably, I grew restless. How long until Crane came home? Whatever room I was in, I looked for a clock. Time had never passed so slowly.

I busied myself with dinner preparations. Homemade biscuits instead of stale white bread, no peanut butter, something special to celebrate, like a cake made with fresh strawberries.

I pulled out my cookbook and got to work.

When Crane finally arrived, Mac was with him. Their grim expressions told me their mission had fallen short of expectations. I made coffee, cut thick slices of cake, and we sat around the table once again.

"They cleared out," Mac said. "Canoe and all. But we found the kid, Rusty Delmar. He's scared."

"He talked," Crane added. "It seems the canoe guys are his cousins. He overheard them planning to kidnap you and Ellalyn Zoller. He didn't know Ellalyn, but he didn't want anything bad to happen to you."

"How about those messages he sent telling me I'd be sorry?"

"He confessed to that. He wanted you to feel bad about not letting him graduate, but he didn't want you dead."

"I guess I should be grateful," I said. "I am."

Someday, I'd look Rusty up and tell him so.

"We'll get the cousins," Mac said. "Maybe not today, but soon we'll have everyone who was in on the plot to kidnap Representative Granville."

"Because of her desire to save the wolves? That's crazy."

"That's not all they're interested in," Mac said. "Basically, they're anti-government. They believe their vision for the future is right, and guns are the only way to achieve it."

"It's a shame Rusty fell for it," I said.

"He idolized his cousin, Claud. Claud promised to give him his heirloom pocket watch as a graduation present."

That wouldn't happen now.

"I still don't understand why they thought I was a danger."

"Rusty knew why. They'd seen you at the farmhouse and with Ellalyn. They thought you were working together."

"Well, I wasn't. Except to find Ellalyn's dog. She thinks stealing Rainbow was part of their plan."

"It was," Mac said. "Claud found a black collie on a farm nearby and switched her with Rainbow, then he turned Rainbow loose."

"Pepper is with Sue Appleton, and Rainbow is still missing."

Having finished his cake, Mac got up. I grabbed his shirt sleeve. "You're not going till you tell us who killed Celia Loring."

"That's a sad story," he said with a teasing glint in his blue eyes. "Are you sure you want to hear it?"

I didn't think that deserved an answer.

"There won't be an arrest," he said. "The killer died ten years ago. He was Marigold Asher's nephew, Jamie, a very disturbed young man. Ms. Asher has been protecting him all these years."

I remembered how Marigold had helped Joanne look for Celia, and how the two women had remained close while Marigold harbored her terrible secret.

"I got a break when I tracked down the guy who drove the ice cream truck. He described Jamie and Celia who were standing in line together that day. Then, when I interviewed Ms. Asher, she admitted Jamie was obsessed with Celia. He told her that he didn't mean to kill Celia. He gave her a shove, she fell and hit her head on a rock. He panicked and ran away."

"Then he came back to the park and buried her body in the woods?"

"Ms. Asher said she didn't want to know any details, but she promised to protect him. As you can guess, Ms. Linder didn't take the news well."

"I wouldn't think so," I said.

Tomorrow or the next day, I would visit her, if she wanted company, that is. To be betrayed by a friend was a special kind of hell. I was fortunate in that all of my friends were true.

~ * ~

It rained the next morning. As soon as the sun came out, I sat on the porch, watching my collies at play. Misty was the first to alert me to company. They came on foot: Molly, Jennifer, Ginger running along the lane, and a tricolor collie on a long lead.

My dogs flew into a barking frenzy. Within minutes, I found myself in the midst of ten collies, all wagging tails, excited yips, and play bows.

"Surprise!" Molly said. "Look who we found!"

I took Rainbow's lead, and she raised her paw to shake hands.

She was a real beauty, with sparkling eyes and the distinctive white collar broken through with glossy black fur. I wished I'd been the one to find her. Well, all that mattered was that she was found.

"So you're Rainbow," I said. "Everybody's been looking for you."

She wagged her tail.

Ignoring the wicker chairs, the girls sat on the stairs,

"Does Ellalyn know?" I asked.

"We just called her," Molly said. "She's coming here to pick up Rainbow and take her home."

"And Mr. Fowler's going to pay us that reward," Jennifer added. "We'll split it. We're saving for college."

Molly said, "Mr. Fowler told us what happened to you. We've been looking for you in the park. Then we found a bag of treats from Pluto's. The next time we saw Rainbow, we were ready. She was good and hungry. Then we heard from Mr. Fowler that you had come home. Then..."

She stopped to take a breath, and Jennifer added, "Who'd have thought Rusty was a hero?"

"Well," I said, then decided to let Rusty keep his 'big man' reputation with the girls.

Again, Misty alerted me to company approaching on the lane. This time Rainbow joined her, crying like a tiny puppy. Rainbow strained on the lead, trying to break free when she saw Ellalyn's car—her car—turn in our driveway.

Ellalyn all but flew out of the car. "Rainbow! Baby! You can let her go, Jennet."

I let the lead fall to the ground, and Rainbow leaped into her mistress' outstretched arms, causing Ellalyn to fall back on the car. She kept her arms around Rainbow and let her tears fall on the collie's head.

"Thank you thank you thank you..."

I felt tears spring into my own eyes. This reunion was the stuff of a Lassie movie, all the more poignant as it might have not happened if not for Molly and Jennifer.

To make the scene perfect, there should be a rainbow in the sky. Why not? We'd had the shower. I looked. Just endless blue, and white clouds floating over Foxglove Corners. Over my home.

Forty-eight

I'm alive!

I reveled in several happy realizations as the sun rose high in the heavens the next day. I was no longer trapped in a farmhouse basement. I could go anywhere and do anything I pleased. It was summer, the sun was bright, and the day was mine.

What did I want to do today? What had I missed most when I was a prisoner?

Crane. My home. I just wanted to play with my precious collies and see my friends. I dreamed of breathing fresh air and gathering flowers from the garden.

Choose a destination, I told myself.

Immediately an image of a lime cooler formed in my mind.

Clovers. Talk to Annica. Visit Ellalyn and Lucy. Go to the library. But don't cram all that into one day.

Some would say my life was dull, but it was the life I wanted. Or they might say I hadn't been a captive that long. When you're deprived of your freedom, though, even an hour is too long.

Candy nudged me and turned her eyes to the Lassie tin on the counter. Taking the hint, I gave the dogs extra biscuits, played with them, and afterward watched them settle down for a mid-morning nap. We all agreed it was too hot to run after a ball.

Later, I slipped on a pastel blue sundress, added a cardigan for air-conditioning, and headed to Crispian Road and Clovers. I thought I'd never see those happy green clovers dancing in the border around the little restaurant again.

For a moment, it seemed as if nothing untoward or terrible had marred the happy summer days.

Then I stepped inside the restaurant to the faint music of the clover chimes and saw a red-haired boy sitting alone in a booth, drinking a Coke. He looked young and vulnerable.

My initial reaction was to retreat until I recalled wanting to see Rusty again to thank him and perhaps gather a little more information about militia activities. I looked directly at him and smiled. He appeared shocked to see me and a bit embarrassed. That was natural, considering our last encounter.

A faint blush stole over his features, and a ghost of a smile answered mine. Gone was the tough guy persona he'd adopted in the park.

"Uh, Mrs. Ferguson," he said. "Nice day, huh?"

"Beautiful." I sat opposite him, not asking permission to do so. "Are you all right now, Rusty?"

"I will be. They got nothing on me."

"I'm happy to hear that. I want to thank you for saving my life."

"Aw, it was nothing."

I smiled. "I don't consider my life nothing."

"Yeah, well, I couldn't let them hurt you or the other lady."

"It took real courage to go against your relatives," I said.

"Well, Claud got carried away. It happens. He's a good guy at heart."

To my knowledge, Claud was still at large, along with his brother and the men named by Ellalyn, but the law's net was wide and far-reaching. I was truly happy to know Rusty wouldn't be caught in it.

"What will you do now?" I asked.

"I'm going to night school in the fall to pick up that credit I need. I'll be okay."

"That's good."

"You were right not to pass me," he said after a while.

Would wonders never cease?

"The night school credit will mean more to you because you'll have earned it," I said. "What did you order?"

"Bacon cheeseburger."

"It's on me."

"You don't have to do that. I got money."

"I want to." I beckoned to Marcy. At the same moment, Annica emerged from the kitchen carrying a tray of desserts for the carousel.

"I see my favorite booth is empty," I said. "I'm going to grab it. Best of luck."

"Hey, thanks!"

I rose as Marcy appeared at Rusty's booth. "This check is on me," I told her.

One bacon cheeseburger with a refill of Coca-Cola. The price of my life.

As planned, I claimed my favorite booth and gazed out the window at the woods on the other side of the road until Annica sauntered up to me with a radiant smile. She made a great show of placing a glass of water in front of me and moving the yellow carnation centerpiece to one side. A flash of deep red sparkled on her finger.

"You have a new ring," I said.

She raised her hand and let the ruby in the circlet of diamonds catch the light, let it drink its full. The jewel brought out the highlights in her red-gold hair.

"Not just any ring. Brent gave it to me."

"Is it an engagement ring then?"

I wasn't really that obtuse, and Annica's announcement wasn't really a surprise. Still, it felt like one. Brent had kept his own counsel, which was a departure for him.

"Brent asked me to marry him last night, and I said 'yes.' I'm so happy!"

Annica was always radiant, but this morning her joy was tangible. It was as if she were encased in light. As if she could shake a pitcher of pure delight over anyone who came in her view.

"When is the wedding?" I asked.

"We haven't set a date. I'm going to finish school, but it's going to happen. The ring says so."

"You realize you're taking Foxglove Corner's premier bachelor out of circulation?"

"I am." She twirled her tiny hot air balloon earring. "I'll confess I wasn't sure he was going to propose until he did." She gave one more admiring glance at her ring. "Are you having lunch?"

"Just a lime cooler."

"I'll join you. Later on, we're going to have a party to celebrate our engagement."

"Are Crane and I invited?

"You certainly are. We want all our friends around us, but you're special, Jennet. I'd never have met Brent if I hadn't met you first. You remember when you came into Past Perfect and I tried to sell you a poisoner's ring?" She sighed. "We've had a lot of fun. A lot of great adventures."

"That won't end," I pointed out. "I'm not going to lose my partner-in-detection."

"You and me and Brent," she said with a smile so bright it lit up the entire restaurant. "And Crane."

I felt as if she had sprinkled fairy dust over my head.

~ * ~

Abandoned no more.

Twin planters filled with pink geraniums flanked Ellalyn's front door, providing a cheery welcome to visitors. The drapes were open, and from inside came high-pitched barking. The barker's faced appeared in the window. Rainbow. Out of sight, her tail would be wagging.

What a difference!

Ellalyn opened the door with a smile that echoed the porch flowers' cheer. Rainbow trotted away from the window and stood at her side.

"Jennet!" she said. "Come in. I've been wanting to touch base with you."

She was having coffee and, apparently, reading the *Banner*, which was spread out on the coffee table next to a vase of red roses. Their rich fragrance filled the air.

Red roses for love.

"I was reading about Claud," she said. "He and his brother were arrested in Kentucky last night."

Ah yes. The long arm of the law. The wide net. The fugitives had headed south down I-75, thinking it would take them to obscurity.

"As Garth would say, justice prevails," she said.

"Garth?"

"Garth MacKay. Did you know he was an informer, too? He suspected Greg belonged to the militia and was in on the plot to kidnap our rep. He's been gathering proof. From now on, it's MacKay Title."

So Garth was at the farmhouse searching for evidence. We had nothing to fear from him. But how could we know he wasn't one of *them*?

"Garth is an amazing man," Ellalyn said.

"If you say so. I don't know him."

"He tracked down the farmer who sold Greg the dog he substituted for my Rainbow."

"Pepper."

"The guy didn't want her back, so he's going to see Sue Appleton about adopting her. How many men would do that?"

"A dog lover," I said, remembering the shepherd in the picture of Garth and his sister.

She seemed suddenly flustered, at a loss for words. "Will you have a piece of cake? It doesn't have peanut butter in it."

I should hope not. I'd never been a fan of peanut butter. After tasting it on stale bread, I planned to boycott it henceforth.

I accepted Ellalyn's offer and sat back while she disappeared into the kitchen. Rainbow followed her. She wasn't about to let Ellalyn out of her sight. I was happy Rainbow was back where she belonged, and Ellalyn had apparently found a new love interest with Greg's partner.

Love is in the air, I thought. *Annica is newly engaged. Ellalyn found a man in an unlikely situation. Miss Eidt is planning her wedding.*

I don't have to bask in others' joy. I have a husband who showers me with attention and sometimes brings me flowers. Sometimes they come from our own gardens, but they're still flowers.

"Tell me more about Garth MacKay," I said when she returned with large slices of German chocolate cake. "I always like a mystery to end in romance."

"Well, I met Garth and Greg at the same time. They were both attractive, but Greg was more outgoing. I liked him right away..."

~ * ~

I took the long way home, savoring the familiar scenery. Woods and lakes and curving country roads. When I reached Jonquil Lane and our green Victorian farmhouse, I had the strangest feeling I was seeing it for the first time. Gleaming gingerbread trim and sunlight dancing on the stained-glass windows between the double gables. The dogs were barking. My life was waiting for me. Dinner to make and dogs to brush and feed, rooms to straighten. Even the most mundane of household chores took on the shine of adventure.

Don't get carried away, Jennet.

That evening, Crane and I sat on the porch watching the stars appear. Our collie family lay in their favorite napping spots with their large water bowl and two bedraggled plush animals. Except for Misty, who had stationed herself at my feet, wide awake and alert.

"It's really over," I said.

"It will be when they catch all the people who were involved in the plot. Until then, I want you to enjoy the rest of the summer in the house and the garden."

I didn't remind him that Evil could find me at home. It knew my address.

"Definitely I won't go to Woodsboro Park again," I said.

What would I do? I thought about it. I'd soon grow tired of cooking and baking, cleaning house, pulling weeds...

"I'll write," I said. "I could add this adventure to my spirit book, except there were no ghosts in it. I didn't do anything except get captured. The girls found Rainbow, and Mac solved the Celia Loring case."

"You're still a heroine in my book," Crane said.

He rose and drew me into his arms for a long kiss.

"Let's turn in."

Anticipating before-bed biscuits, Candy raised her head. I took one last look at the starry sky and let Crane lead me inside. It had been a long day.

Meet Dorothy Bodoin

Dorothy Bodoin lives in Royal Oak, Michigan, an hour's drive from the little town that inspired Foxglove Corners. Dorothy worked as a secretary for Chrysler Missile Corporation, two years of which were spent in southern Italy. A graduate of Oakland University with bachelor's and master's degrees in English literature, she taught English for several years at Madison High School in Michigan. On retiring from teaching, she began her second career as a writer. She is the author of the Foxglove Corners mystery series, six novels of romantic suspense, and one Gothic romance.

The Snow Dogs of Lost Lake - A ghostly white collie and a lost locket lead Jennet Greenway to a body in the woods and a dangerous new mystery. (#6)

The Collie Connection - As Jennet Greenway's wedding to Crane Ferguson approaches, her happiness is shattered when a Good Samaritan deed leaves her without her beloved black collie, Halley, and ultimately in grave danger. (#7)

A Time of Storms - When a stranger threatens her collie and she hears a cry for help in a vacant house, Jennet Ferguson suspects that her first summer as a wife may be tumultuous. (#8)

The Dog from the Sky - Jennet's life takes a dangerous turn when she rescues an abused collie. Soon afterward, a girl vanishes without a trace. Ironically she had also rescued an abused collie. Is there a connection between the two incidents? (#9)

Spirit of the Season - Mystery mixes with holiday cheer as a phantom ice skater returns to the lake where she died, and a collie is accused of plotting her owner's fatal accident. (#10)

Another Part of the Forest - Danger rides the air when a kidnapper whisks his victims away in a hot air balloon, and a false friend puts a curses on a collie breeder's first litter. (#11)

Where Have All the Dogs Gone? - An animal activist frees the shelter dogs in and around Foxglove Corners to save them from being destroyed. Running wild in the countryside, they face an equally distressing fate and post a risk to those who come in contact with them. (#12)

The Secret Room of Eidt House - A rabid dog that should have died months ago from the dread disease runs free in the woods of Foxglove Corners, and the library's long-kept secret unleashes a series of other strange events. (#13)

Follow a Shadow - A shadowy intruder haunts Jennet's woods by night, and a woman who can't accept the death of her collie asks Jennet to help her find Rainbow Bridge where she believes her dog waits for her. (#14)

The Snow Queen's Collie - A white collie puppy appears on the porch of the Ferguson farmhouse during a Christmas Eve snowstorm. In another part of Foxglove Corners a collie breeder's show prospect disappears. Meanwhile, the painting Jennet's sister gave her for Christmas begins to exhibit strange qualities. (#15)

The Door in the Fog - A wounded dog disappears in the fog. A blue door on the side of a barn vanishes. Strange wildflowers and a sound of weeping haunt a meadow. The woods keep their secret, and a curse refuses to die. (#16)

Dreams and Bones - At Brent Fowler's newly purchased Spirit Lamp Inn, a renovation turns up human bones buried in the inn's backyard, rekindling interest in the case of a young woman who disappeared from the inn several decades ago. As Jennet tries to solve this mystery, she doesn't realize it may be her last. (#17)

A Ghost of Gunfire - Months after gunfire erupted in her classroom at Marston High School, leaving one student dead and one seriously wounded, Jennet begins to hear a sound of gunshots inaudible to anyone else. Meanwhile, she resolves to find the demented person who is tying dogs to trees and leaving them to die. (#18)

The Silver Sleigh - Rosalyn Everett was missing and presumed dead. Her collies had been rescued, and her house was abandoned. But a blue merle collie haunts her woods and a figure in bridal white traverses the property. (#19)

The Stone Collie - Jennet's discovery of a collie puppy chained in the yard of a vacant house sets her on a search for a man whose activities may threaten Foxglove Corners' security. Meanwhile, horror story novelist Lucy Hazen is mystified when scenes from her work-in-progress are duplicated in real life. (#20)

The Mists of Huron Court - The house was beautiful, a vintage pink Victorian in a picturesque but lonely country setting, and the girl playing ball with her dog in the yard was friendly, suggesting that she and Jennet walk their dogs together some time. Jennet thinks she has made a new friend until she returns to the house and finds a tumbling down ruin where the Victorian once stood and no sign that the girl and dog have ever been there. ((#21)

Down a Dark Path - What hold does the pink Victorian on Huron Court have on Brent Fowler who is determined to re-create the home of long-dead Violet Randall? When he disappears, could he have been cast adrift in time? (#22))

Shadow of the Ghost Dog - An invisible dog grieves inside the house chosen as a setting for the movie based on Lucy Hazen's book *Devilwish*, and a landscaper unearths a human skeleton in the backyard while planting shrubs. (#23))

The Dark Beyond the Bridge - The discovery of a secret ghost town in a densely rural area of Michigan's lower peninsula leads to mystery and danger for Jennet Ferguson and her friends. (#24)

The Deadly Fields of Autumn - An antique television set that airs an obscure Western at random times and a woman who disappears with her newly-adopted rescue dog draw Jennet into a puzzling mystery. (#25)

The Lost Collies of Silverhedge - Collie breeder Madselin Rivard was dead, leaving her prized, valuable collies uncared for in their kennel. Jennet and her friends rescue five of them, but eight remain unaccounted for. (#26)

All the Pretty Little Collies - Danger stalks the collies of Foxglove Corners when an unknown villain begins tossing poisoned meat into their yards, and a girl with a winning blue merle collie is warned via threatening messages to withdraw her dog from competition or risk the consequences. (#27)

Phantom in the Pond - Brent Fowler's plan to open a house for geriatric collies goes awry when strange things begin to happen in his newly-purchased country estate. (#28)

Challenge a Scarecrow - Scarecrows that guard a dangerous secret and a woman who believes she has brought her dog back to life add up to a frightening and deadly month for Jennet Ferguson. (#29)

The Dog Who Ran with the Sleigh - The apparition of an old-fashioned horse-drawn sleigh on a snowy road sends Jennet Ferguson over a deep slope into danger and possible death. (#30)

In the Greenwood He Was Slain - A search for four collie puppies abandoned on a country lane leads Jennet to a mysterious house in the woods, and a story of love, betrayal, and murder. (#31)

Letter to Our Readers

Enjoy this book?

You can make a difference

As an independent publisher, Wings ePress, Inc. does not have the financial clout of the large New York Publishers. We can't afford large magazine spreads or subway posters to tell people about our quality books.

But, we do have something much more effective and powerful than ads. We have a large base of loyal readers.

Honest Reviews help bring the attention of new readers to our books.

If you enjoyed this book, we would appreciate it if you would spend a few minutes posting a review on the site where you purchased this book or on the Wings ePress, Inc. webpages at:
https://wingsepress.com/

Visit Our Website

For The Full Inventory
Of Quality Books:

Wings ePress.Inc
https://wingsepress.com/

Quality trade paperbacks and downloads
in multiple formats,
in genres ranging from light romantic comedy
to general fiction and horror.
Wings has something for every reader's taste.
Visit the website, then bookmark it.
We add new titles each month!

Wings ePress Inc.
3000 N. Rock Road
Newton, KS 67114